David Telfair

St. Martin's Press, New York

Design by Karin Batten

Library of Congress Cataloging-in-Publication Data

Telfair, David.
Cherton / David Telfair.
p. cm.
ISBN 0-312-02883-0
I. Title.
PR6070.E39C48 1989
823′.914—dc19

89-4134
CIP

First Edition

10 9 8 7 6 5 4 3 2 1

TO

Charles Lanier Nowlin, Jr.

''Elinor agreed to it all, for she did not think he deserved the compliment of rational opposition.''

—Jane Austen
Sense and Sensibility

"Cherton," of course,
rhymes with "Barton."

Introduction

According to such publications as see fit to mention it, Cherton, in the County of Wroxshire, is a tiny village (population 421) some miles north of Oxford. The more critical tourist, should he happen to find himself in Cherton, is likely to suspect that the figure of 421 has been eked out with recruits from the local churchyard. Certainly it is true that it might require a vision more than ordinarily acute to distinguish some of the present-day villagers from the remains of their forebears resting beneath St. Margaret's tidily tended sod.

There seems to be no good for Cherton's existence. True, there was once a Benedictine abbey nearby, but the village itself was a center for neither wool nor beer; it was not even a market town. It has never been on or near a main route. Even today Cherton is almost inaccessible; to have reached it by horse or carriage must have required the courage and acuity of one of the more enterprising conquistadors.

For a few years in the second quarter of the sixteenth century, Cherton was the seat of Sir Robert Woodley, a former mayor of the village. He had displayed laudable activity in persuading the local ecclesiastics (by various interesting methods) to remove themselves from the district. In gratitude, the appreciative Henry VIII conferred a knighthood upon the Hammer of the Monks, who proceeded to convert the abbey into a quarry, erecting the earliest portion of the handsome sprawling house that today is Mauley Hall. Regrettably, Queen Mary and Sir Robert did not see eye to eye on monastic matters, and Sir Robert was duly roasted alive at Smithfield in 1556. In 1562, Queen Elizabeth I rehabilitated his memory, restoring the manor (although not its revenues) to the widowed Lady Woodley.

Sir Robert was Cherton's sole contribution to history, but

during his brief period of prosperity, a certain amount of architectural activity occurred, and much of the charm of the village lies in the quaint buildings, public and private.

About the year 1690, Lord Mauley, the great-grandson of Sir Robert, retired from Court at the earnest request of King William. His presence in the village caused another spurt of building that lasted well into the 1730s. A possible explanation for this is that Lord Mauley had established a brickyard on part of his property and was anxious to encourage the local economy. Evidently, this caused some problems, for there is, in the local records, an entry for the year 1708 referring to one James Perryfytte, "a vile, lowe Wretch, thot to bee a conceal'd Papist butt that not prov'd," who was imprisoned for insolence to Lord Mauley. James, it appears, had refused to demolish his stone dwelling and replace it with one of the infinitely more desirable brick.

The rest of the eighteenth century and all of the nineteenth is a somewhat dreary chronicle of the comings and goings of the various Lords Mauley and their guests, the Lords Thicester and the Dukes of Thatshire. One bright spot is the Third Viscount, who went hopelessly mad in 1791, spending the remaining thirty years of his life under the mistaken but ineradicable impression that he was Zenobia, Queen of Palmyra.

As late as 1900, the village (which had never really been alive) was still contriving to give a reasonably convincing imitation of a cleverly embalmed dummy. Nothing in the guidebook indicates that it has changed much in the last seventy-odd years except for a slight influx of Londoners fleeing the Blitz. The most striking result of that influx was the decision of some of the refugees to remain in Cherton—even after they learned what it was like. As has been said more than once, Cherton is a charming place, but when that has been said—even once—there is little to add.

1

The bachelor owner of Mauley Hall, Charles Alistair Wentworth Woodley, Fifth Baron Pelham, Seventh Viscount Mauley, would not be considered an American film director's idea of a British peer. With his protruding eyes, thick lips, and bald head, over which were halfheartedly brushed a few strands of yellowish-white hair, Lord Mauley was rather a dismal subject. Those sloppy hairs spread about his crown were typical of him. Sometimes in London he had himself fitted for a wig but he could never bring himself to buy one. Probably, he thought, no one noticed his thinning thatch. Actually people did, but no one cared. He could have worn a Lord Fauntleroy wig and the villagers would have done no more than yawn.

It is to be feared that many considered Lord Mauley a bore. Indeed, it is to be feared that a perceptive minority considered him a fool. Certainly his mother did. Emily, Lady Mauley, had spent thirty excruciating years in Cherton, but upon the death of her husband, she had removed, with almost indecent celerity, to Maulcaster House, a safe ninety miles farther north. Her visits to Mauley Hall were as infrequent and as brief as she could contrive them to be.

Lord Mauley opened his eyes and shuddered. He had just remembered Mrs. Staine's invitation. He looked at the clock. It was nearly eight. Slowly he reached for the bellpull at the head of the bed. Then he closed his eyes and meditated.

"Yes, sir?" asked Birkett, who had softly entered the room in response to the summons.

Lord Mauley opened his eyes.

"Oh—good morning, Birkett."

"Good morning, sir. Did you sleep well, sir?"

"Umm? Oh. Yes. Yes, I—I think I did. Ah—is it a nice day, Birkett?"

"Very pleasant, sir. Quite clear and warm for March."

"March? Yes."

Birkett, who earned every penny of his wages, twisted inwardly, but his face remained impassive.

"Shall I draw your bath, sir?"

"Bath?" asked Lord Mauley, as if he were being offered a totally new experience.

"Yes, sir. Your—bath, sir."

"No. No, I don't think I shall have a bath this morning, Birkett." Lord Mauley paused, ruminating. Then he said, "Birkett, I want you to send a note to the vicarage."

"Very well, sir."

"I should like you to send it at once, Birkett."

"Yes, sir. At once, sir."

"Very good, Birkett. I don't think I'll get up quite yet. That will be all for now, Birkett."

Birkett stared at his employer as Lord Mauley shut his eyes and turned onto his side.

"Lord Mauley?"

"Nothing more, Birkett, thank you. Just send the note."

Birkett swallowed.

"Of course, sir. Ah—where is it, sir?"

Lord Mauley sighed. He felt quite sleepy.

"Where is what, Birkett?" he asked. Why didn't the man go away?

Birkett swallowed again.

"The note, sir. The note you wish to send to the vicarage."

"Oh. Don't you have it?"

"No—sir."

"Umm. Oh, yes. Yes. I'll have to write it, won't I?"

Not for the first time did Birkett wrestle with the desire to kick and scream. He did not venture to reply.

Lord Mauley slowly got up from the bed and Birkett handed him the dressing gown and slippers. As Lord Mauley seated himself at his writing table, he looked up at Birkett.

"I'm not at home today, Birkett," he said. "If anyone asks for me, just say I've gone up to London."

"Very well, sir. Shall I tell them to order the car?"

"No, no, no, Birkett! I'm not *really* going, you know. I just want people to *think* that I've gone. If people think that I'm in *London,* they won't think that I'm *here,* will they?"

"Ah—no, sir."

Lord Mauley wrote for a few moments.

"There," he said. "Send that to Mrs. Staine."

"At once, sir."

Lord Mauley meditated again.

"You know, Birkett, as long as I'm up, I suppose I may as well have my tea."

"Very well, sir. I'll send it up at once," said Birkett, edging toward the door.

"Do that, Birkett. I think that I really want my tea."

"Yes, sir," said Birkett, shutting the door.

"So much better *here* than *there,*" muttered Lord Mauley. He returned to the bed, congratulating himself upon this example of social guile. It was, he thought, *so* important to keep appearances as they should be. He meditated still further, turning over in his mind this estimable attitude. Suddenly he gave a slight start.

Is it? he wondered.

Then he shook his head and shut his eyes. He was just dozing off when Whittaker entered with the tray.

2

Certainly Mr. Staine was not to blame for his face; it was a natural liability. At first glance, the Vicar of St. Margaret's, Cherton, Wrox., (population 421), gave the impression of pure intellect, of razor-sharp perception. Ten minutes of his society were generally enough to persuade all but the most obtuse that the vicar's brain had little in common with his appearance. That narrow scholar's face, those piercing bright-blue eyes, those thin sensitive lips, that impressive silver hair were so many stage props. Like stage props, those assets deceived only the sympathetic observer. The most amiable suspension of disbelief on the part of even a moderately alert parishioner could do no more than convince him that the incumbent of St. Margaret's was a well-meaning ass. The more astute caught glimpses of certain characteristics and attitudes that were as unfortunate as they were unexpected in a man of Mr. Staine's profession.

Chance had sent him to Oxford, and chance had thrown him (the verb is not inapt) into the Church. Chance had likewise obligingly provided him with a wife wholly fitted to his requirements. Lela Staine was not clever, and, unlike her husband, she looked as dense as she was. Occasionally, strangers would marvel that so intelligent a man should have married so silly a woman, but that was only until they knew the vicar better.

Many who knew him felt that his incumbency was a disaster without remedy. His social equals tried to believe that the constricted society of the village forced them to observe the amenities of polite intercourse. Those luckier parishioners not on visiting terms with the vicarage were as outspoken to their fellow plebeians as they were discreet with their "betters." Jennifer Simms, the Staines' long-suffering maid-of-all-work, was the frequent recipient of sincere compassion and hypocritically solicitous inquiries as to the well-being of the "bloody parson" and his winsome wife.

Miss Granby, on the other hand, was an intellectual. She read books. She could talk about the very latest novelists, poets, and philosophers, and if she couldn't make *you* understand, she at least gave the impression that *she* knew what she was talking about. She was in her mid-forties, dark-haired and pretty, and she had the knack of appearing to think about what she was saying. She was terribly advanced and broad-minded. Naturally, she impressed the vicar and his wife (although not always favorably).

Miss Granby had read psychology at the University of Delaware (in the States), and most of the village society regarded her with awe and distrust. Of course, this was only to be expected. Miss Granby thought nothing of using such words as *syphilis* and *homosexual* at the vicarage tea table. She subscribed to *Encounter*. Her chief literary trophy was a photograph of Jean Genet, upon which she had inscribed *à ma chère Françoise*. She had once, some years back, been heard asking Lord Mauley to contribute to a fund for the Cambridge education of a stateside Black Muslim. (Lord Mauley had been unable to understand why black muslin—or any other color—should be sent to Cambridge, and Miss Granby had retired in bafflement.)

Lord Mauley's nearest neighbor and most distant acquaintance was Dr. Stephen Robbertson, who occupied a small house with a view of the Hall gates and their ramping supporters. Dr. Robbertson was a well-built slender man of forty-seven, who had settled in Cherton some years after the close of the war. No one in the village had yet been able to discover just what sort of doctor he was. The doctor himself had learned that it had been put about the village that he was a defrocked cleric of dubious background. This, he knew, was the work of the vicar. He knew also that Portia Hitchcock had confided to Miss Granby that he was an ex-don, expelled from one of the universities for Unmentionable Practices. Dr. Robbertson had not seen fit to clarify the situation, for it gave him too much satisfaction. In his bedroom, there hung the gloriously engrossed certificate of his doctorate, a distinction he had achieved at the age of seventeen, thanks to a mail-order course in veterinary science. He enjoyed enormously the aura of mystery and the pleasure of pulling the assorted legs of Cherton society.

Dr. Robbertson, the recipient of a comfortable income, played near-champion tennis and was an excellent swimmer. His principal amusement indoors (contrary to the suspicions of some of his neighbors) was painting. His competent copies of mid-Georgian portraits were painted, he once said, because he liked to reproduce the different textures of satin, velvet, lace, and flesh. His landscapes of the early twentieth-century English school were equally good, but his most profitable works—and those that had provoked the greatest comment—were life studies (exclusively male) of a photographic and startling anatomical exactitude.

He was seldom seen in the village except on weekends when he appeared in the bar of the Rose Revived with one of his models in tow. The model varied, but his type seldom did: twentyish, slim, with dark wavy hair, lean-loined and wide-shouldered. Dr. Robbertson cared nothing for gossip, but he enjoyed knowing that he was the cause of it. He was popular with the villagers, and the publican would not have dared to hint that the doctor's custom would have been more welcome without such a blatant display of leather-jacketed masculinity.

Because he found Cherton a pretty and inexpensive place to live, Dr. Robbertson remained there, but frequent trips to London and the Continent were essential to his sanity. There were few of his social peers whom he could tolerate for much longer than thirty minutes, although he had a shy admiration for Miss Granby. She amused him, and he suspected that he might amuse her. Perhaps, au fond, she was as much of a rebel as he. He often thought he would like to find out, but he felt it would require more than the everyday inanities of Cherton society to provoke a genuine attempt at intimacy. Furthermore, other complications had recently entered his life.

Mr. and Mrs. Thomas Hitchcock generally deplored the village. A general deploration was a way of life with them. Thomas Hitchcock had spent his early youth in India when empire building was still a respectable occupation. When it became evident that the white man's burden was shifting to other, darker shoulders, he left palm for pine and returned to

England, pausing only at Port Said to marry Portia Hampden, whom he had met at a missionary tea. He had been a fool to marry Miss Hampden. Unfortunately, he was not fool enough to be happy with her. A reasonably clever man, he had taken refuge in a pompous bitterness, a constant puzzle to his wife.

Miss Hampden had been an early product of St. Hugh's, where she had not achieved a First in Ancient History. Mr. Hitchcock had read Greek at Cambridge, so there was a certain amount of common ground for what they later were to call their connubial jocundity. Only the most imaginative could have envisaged such a state *chez* Hitchcock. Thomas, square-jawed, mustachioed, and squat, looked like a cartoonist's idea of a Prussian officer. Portia Hitchcock, short-chinned, hawk-beaked, and emaciated, was known locally as "Dracula's Daughter."

It is to be supposed, however, that each had talents of a sort for the marriage and that no just impediment had yet marred the romantic obligations contracted in the Consulate at Port Said. Their interests were few. Portia prided herself upon her greenhouses and kept the drawing room filled with flowers. Thomas wrote occasional letters to the *Times* (one was once even published), worked on his annotated edition of *Cranford,* and made almost daily additions to his already enormous collection of gramophone records. Both aspired to seeing their delightful house (rented from Lord Mauley on rather peculiar terms) one day displayed in *Country Life.* The likelihood was remote.

It was *Country Life* that had rendered the widowed Mrs. James Dodridge so complacent (at least so believed the Hitchcocks). Twice—and there was every possibility of a third occasion—Mrs. Dodridge's gem of an early-Georgian house had appeared in the sacred pages. The Adam drawing room with the Kauffmann ceiling, the Zoffany portrait of Miss Caroline Dodridge, the Gainsborough portrait of

Lady Elizabeth du Belamant, the Tompion clocks, the Tabel harpsichord, the original (if somewhat battered) toile hangings of the principal bedchamber, the grounds by Brown, all, all had graced the glossy pages of that estimable periodical.

That Mrs. Dodridge was complacent is not to be doubted, but let it not be thought that her complacency extended to the rudeness of superiority of manner. Although the daughter and (now) the elder sister of a duke, she had never chosen to call herself Lady Julia. As Mrs. James Dodridge, she was content, and if she looked down her delicately pointed nose at Lord Mauley, surely that was a foible harmless enough. She was, perhaps, less broad-minded and tolerant than she liked to think herself, but she bore with the vicar, laughed at his wife, and was decently courteous to the Hitchcocks. To have asked more would have been irrational.

3

"Frederick! That tea yesterday!" Mrs. Staine was disturbed.

"Yes, my dear? The tea?"

"I don't think I liked that tea! Is that what we ordered from Fortnum's?"

The vicar considered in a clerical way.

"It tasted all right to me. What's wrong with it?"

"It tasted like Assam. I dislike Assam, you know, even more than Congou. It's supposed to be Darjeeling."

"I can't tell one from the other, my dear," said the vicar.

His wife sighed in exasperation.

"No, I don't suppose you can, but *I* can, and I'm *sure* it's Assam."

The vicar sighed in turn.

"Well, I dare say the others won't notice anything. It tasted all right to me. They won't know."

"No," said his wife, "but *I* shall. I *do so* loathe Assam!"

"It tasted all right to me," said the vicar.

"Frederick, if you say that once more, I shall scream!"

"Say what?"

"Say that it's all right. It's *not* all right! I *loathe* Assam!"

"They won't notice anything, I'm sure. It tasted all—"

"Frederick!"

"Oh, very well. Who's coming, by the way?"

"The usual crowd. The Hitchcocks, Fanny Granby, Dr. Robbertson, Mrs. Dodridge. I asked Lady Thelma, but she's engaged—she *said.*"

The vicar frowned.

"Isn't Lord Mauley coming?" he asked.

"Lord Mauley," replied his wife, "sent a note saying that he found it necessary to go up to London."

She sounded bitter.

"You sound bitter," observed the vicar.

"I *am* bitter. He knows perfectly well that I wanted him here to counteract the Hitchcocks. He could have gone up to London another day."

The vicar pondered.

"Perhaps he forgot, Lela."

"*Forgot?* How could he *possibly* have forgotten if he remembered to send a note?"

"I mean perhaps he forgot when he accepted."

"Hardly. He was asked only yesterday."

"Oh."

The vicar yawned.

"It's four o'clock," he said. "What time are they to be here?"

"I said 'around four,'" said his wife. "They should be here soon."

The vicar yawned again.

"I hope they're not too long about it."

"About what?" Mrs. Staine was very irritated.

"About—there's the bell now. Do you suppose it's they?"

The pair listened as they heard Simms go into the passage. They heard the front door open, and a subdued racket of murmured civilities leaked into the drawing room. Mr. and Mrs. Staine rose from their chairs and faced the double mahogany doors with rigid smiles of social grace.

The Hitchcocks came in, followed by Dr. Robbertson, who looked about hopefully for Miss Granby. Mrs. Hitchcock gave her celebrated laugh.

"Oh, are we the first? We *always* are! I suppose because we live farthest away. So *nice* to see you, dear Lela. *Dear* Mr. Staine! So *nice* to see you again!"

Dr. Robbertson's eyes, slightly prominent and of a startlingly dark blue, pulsed in his head as he stood near the door waiting for his turn. He stared at the others. He thought, What a quartet! Old Hitchcock is looking profound and earnest as usual. Hard to tell what he sees—or doesn't see—behind those thick green spectacles. And listen to *her*! How can anyone but the Staines try to carry on a conversation with the woman?

Mrs. Staine moved a step toward the doctor.

"Dr. Robbertson! I'm *so* glad you could come! It's been *quite* a while since we've seen you here, you know. It's really very *naughty* of you."

The vicar joined in.

"Indeed it *is,* Doctor! You've *quite* neglected us!"

Now why, thought the doctor, does he find it necessary to drop his voice a fifth in pitch? You'd think he was in his damned pulpit!

Dr. Robbertson took a breath and plunged in.

"Yes, I suppose I have. But, you know, this is such a sleepy little place that time goes by without one's noticing it. One's never really sure whether he's awake or asleep."

Would that *do*? he wondered. No, old Dracula's Daughter's going to pick up the ball.

Indeed, Mrs. Hitchcock was anxious to speak before the doctor had finished.

"Why, Dr. Robbertson! You *are* naughty! Really, I don't know *how* you can call Cherton sleepy! It seems to me that there's *always* something to talk about!"

"There would be even if there weren't," said the doctor gloomily. Then he cheered up as he realized that he had temporarily derailed Portia Hitchcock's one-track mind. And a monorail at that, he thought.

In the dull lull following the doctor's remark, the hostess got them into chairs and rang for tea. (*Was* it Darjeeling?) The doorbell sounded.

"Ah," said the vicar, looking benignly about, "the doorbell."

"There must be someone at the door," his wife confided to no one in particular.

Dr. Robbertson repressed an impulse to leap from his chair and strangle the woman. Even the Hitchcocks had the glassy look that comes from trying to remain expressionless.

Mrs. Dodridge was ushered in, and the three gentlemen rose like so many startled pheasants.

The vicar went gallantly forward. His voice, Dr. Robbertson noted with increased irritation, was nearly an octave deeper.

With an implacable jollity, Mr. Staine shepherded the newcomer across the room. Dr. Robbertson could bear it no longer.

"Why, Vicar!" he exclaimed. "You sound like Father Christmas!"

Mrs. Dodridge later recalled the vicar's expression as one of the few pleasures the afternoon had afforded, and she took advantage of his temporary muteness to get in her licks.

"So pleasant to come, Mrs. Staine. Hello, Portia, Thomas. A lovely afternoon, isn't it? Dr. Robbertson, so pleasant! I hope you've had no further trouble with your central heating?"

The doctor replied civilly enough that he hadn't. Mrs. Dodridge meant well, but he did wish she wouldn't throw conversational topics so recklessly about. To do the woman justice, perhaps she was too sensible to realize just what was considered a conversational topic in the Cherton beau monde, although, God knew, experience should have told her. As he expected, the Hitchcock was eyeing him with what she doubtless supposed was an alert and sympathetic interest. Actually, she looked as if she was suffering from a severe toothache and smiling to conceal it.

"You've had trouble with your central heating, Doctor? One *really* can't trust these *modern* conveniences, *can* one?"

The doctor, who knew that for years the Hitchcocks had been trying to induce Lord Mauley to install central heating in their house, ventured to release his tongue from between his teeth.

"Only a clogged fuel line. Nothing serious, but it took the chap a long time to find it."

For the first time since his arrival, Mr. Hitchcock spoke.

"Rather expected to see Fanny Granby with us this afternoon."

"Indeed you will, Mr. Hitchcock! You know, she's always a little—um—*en retard,* as our friends across that—ah, insidious Channel say, but she'll be here. Oh, *yes* indeed!"

And the vicar smiled, conscious of having achieved just the right touch of reassuring suavity.

Thomas Hitchcock stirred his tea, peering into the cup as if an answer might be lurking there. He was trying to think of something that would satisfactorily deflate the vicar. He tasted the tea. Darjeeling—one of his favorites. Here was an opening—a trifle gauche, but it would serve.

"You always have such excellent tea, my dear Mrs. Staine. Now this is a really superior Assam."

Concentrating on the teapot and wondering whether she should order more toast, Mrs. Staine muttered her gratitude. Her husband felt that more could be had from the subject.

"Your sense of taste must be as keen as Lela's. *I* can't tell *what* I'm drinking."

Mrs. Dodridge thoroughly disapproved of this public evaluation of the refreshments, but she felt that she should contribute something. She tasted her tea critically, then turned to Mr. Hitchcock as the doorbell rang.

"Of course," she said, with what she hoped was an engaging smile, "of course, I know *you* wouldn't make a mistake, you who lived in India, but *I* should have thought this to be Darjeeling."

The doctor was terrified to see that Portia Hitchcock was cranking up her mind to come to her husband's defense. Mercifully, Miss Granby entered the room at that moment, and Assam and Darjeeling died quietly in midair.

"Hello, everyone! Lela, dear, I *know* I'm late! So sorry! That dreary train simply *crawled* to Porford. Please, everyone, do sit down. Oh, may I sit here by you, Mr. Hitchcock? Charming. Tea? Oh, lovely! No sugar and just a drop from the cream jug. My dears, London is *absolutely* unbelievable!"

And Miss Granby sat back and waited for her tea.

Resolutely, Mrs. Dodridge asked why London was unbelievable.

"The crowds, my dear Mrs. Dodridge! *Surely* you haven't forgotten that the President is in London today! Just *swarms* of people!"

The vicar tried to look interested.

"Did you see the President?" he asked.

Miss Granby shook her head with an archly reproving smile.

"Now, Vicar, do I really give the idea of a lion hunter? Only a very *personal* matter of the most *pressing* concern could have persuaded me to quit our dear Cherton for the horrors of a State Visit. Too, *too,* tiresome!"

Nobody felt equal to asking what had taken her to London, and she decided that she had used a phrase miscalculated to make her listeners feel it politer to restrain their curiosity. In this, Miss Granby was mistaken. There was no curiosity, only the general paralysis of mind and body that usually descended upon the Staines' guests after the first thirty minutes of any visit. (When, several days later, Mrs. Dodridge learned from her brother that Miss Granby had been seen in Oxford Street sitting upon a pillar-box and waving a small American flag, she felt doubly repaid for her self-restraint.)

Dr. Robbertson was the first to leave, and by half-past five the Staines were left alone to tell each other how successful the little gathering had been.

Mrs. Staine went to the pantry as soon as the last desperate guest had departed. Fortnum's label was quite legible: DARJEELING.

4

Lady Thelma Mullen, relict of the late Edward Cavendish Mullen, Q.C., often wondered why she lived in Cherton. She was a sensible woman in her late thirties. She played an excellent game of bridge, she enjoyed the theater without finding it necessary to talk about it, she liked music to the extent that she did not attend concerts unless interested in the program, and she had a horror of catchwords and the jargon of fashionable critics and reviewers that amounted to an affliction. Her favorite remark was "I don't have time to be intellectual." She read the *Times* ("I adore the personals!"), that paper's admirable *Literary Supplement* ("Wonderful for the adrenal glands!"), and the *Guardian*. Magazines such as those beloved of Miss Granby left her unmoved, and Lady Thelma was more likely to be found reading Sayers or Tolkien than the profounder effusions of the brighter (and angrier) young men. In her own words, "I seem to be incapable of reading modern novelists; those forthright Danish magazines are preferable, I think." Many writers, she felt, were obsessed by the need for spelling out, in the most sordid and boring terms possible, the age-old obvious. "They have," she once said, "cleverly discovered that we live in a very complex and a very nasty world. They wear their hearts on their sleeves and bare their psyches (as well as other things) with a promiscuity I find distasteful. It's all very well, I dare say, to write intelligently of cruelty, injustice, oppression, corruption, violence, and unconventional sexual habits, but, really, is it necessary to pretend that one has *invented* them?"

Upon another occasion, Lady Thelma had lamented the decline of taste, for she considered taste and beauty synonymous. "Michelangelo, Titian, Shakespeare, Milton, Molière, and all the rest wrote or painted for the taste of their day. And they produced beauty. What has become of beauty, to say nothing of taste? I can see beauty in *Lear* or *Phèdre*. Am I supposed to find it in *Steambath* or *The Best Little Whorehouse in Texas*?"

The morning following the Staines' tea party, Lady Thelma was having coffee with Mrs. Dodridge in the latter's pretty little garden room, where Mrs. Dodridge had been describing the previous afternoon's festivities.

"I simply lied and said I had an engagement," Lady Thelma confessed. "I haven't recovered from the last time yet."

Mrs. Dodridge frowned at her cup and pressed her lips together.

"You look rather grim, Julia," said Lady Thelma with a laugh.

"Possibly I do. Thelma—why do we put up with them? Why do we tolerate those people at the vicarage? Why don't we just leave—since they won't? Just go where people aren't such, well—fools."

"You'd never leave this house, Julia; you know you wouldn't."

"No, I suppose not, although very often I should like to. Especially after one of our neighborly entertainments. Really, have you *ever* seen anyone else like Lela Staine?"

"Certainly. Portia Hitchcock."

"There! That's exactly what I mean! Where else but Cherton could you find two people like that? And the husbands! They're simply their wives' male counterparts. You'd think that two utter negatives might make a positive, but no. Each merely reinforces the worst qualities of the other." Mrs. Dodridge shook her head and then added, "How do you suppose people become like the Staines, Thelma? Heredity is important, I suppose, but—"

Lady Thelma frowned.

"I don't think we can blame heredity entirely for the Staines' charms. You must remember that both have had years of practice—and in each other's society. No one could become like them just overnight."

"They're so very impossible that I've often wondered if they're not really pretending. Yet to what end?"

"Yes, Julia. It's difficult to believe that, if their stupidity is genuine, they could have ever survived—well, the ordinary hazards of infancy and childhood. You know. Things like crossing the road or not drinking from bottles marked POISON."

"Yes, or being pushed down a well by their parents, for that matter. Oh, Thelma, I *wish* that man would get another living! Preferably in Australia."

Lady Thelma extended her cup for more coffee, wrinkling her forehead.

"What Cherton needs, Julia, is some new blood. Some fresh infusion of—of *something*. We've become so flat and unprofitable."

Mrs. Dodridge looked unconvinced.

"I don't know," she said. "I think Cherton absorbs personalities the way China is said to have absorbed her invaders. No. I think that we need some kind of shock treatment or operation. Not a lobotomy, perhaps, but something to rearrange our ways and ideas. Something to produce some kind of new and probably totally unexpected reaction."

"You sound almost technical, Julia!" exclaimed Lady Thelma, smiling. "We certainly do have rich materials for catalysis, but who could come within shrieking distance of our fellow villagers and not become as Chertonesque as they are? Or as *we* are, if it comes to that."

Mrs. Dodridge shrugged.

"*I* can't think of anyone, can you?"

Lady Thelma looked thoughtful.

"No, not really—unless—" Then she shook her head. "No."

"Oh, well!" Mrs. Dodridge pondered. "You know, I've often wondered how much Thomas Hitchcock *really* knows about music."

Lady Thelma snorted.

"I think he knows a great deal about gramophone records but very little about music. I used to think he had an enormously catholic taste. I've since decided that he has merely an enormously catholic record library and a total lack of discrimination. Indeed, I suspect him of being partially tone-deaf. Did you ever hear him try to sing along with the gramophone? But, of course, it makes him happy to be regarded as the Great Cham of music—and it *does* take people in. It took *me* in for years."

"Aren't you being rather harsh, Thelma?"

"Possibly, but I doubt it. You know as well as I do that there is a vast difference between genuine tolerance or forbearance and a brainlessly goody-goody unperceptiveness. I *don't* like fools, and I dislike poseurs even more."

"Like Fanny Granby?" asked Mrs. Dodridge with a mischievious grin.

"Well, Fanny at least has the merit, I suspect, of knowing what a fraud she is. That ridiculous Genet photograph! . . . And, of course, Stephen Robbertson isn't bad at all, Julia."

"Poor Robbie! No, he isn't too bad—especially if you contrast him with the Staines and the Hitchcocks."

"Well, that's scarcely fair. *Anyone* would seem intelligent through such a comparison as that! Besides, I think you're being patronizing, Julia. He's popular, you know—except, perhaps, when he unsettles the Rose! *Where* does he find those extraordinary young men?"

"London, I dare say."

"They're pretty, aren't they, Julia?"

"Umph! Do you know, Robbie once told me—with a perfectly straight face—that he'd made more than sixteen thousand pounds from their pictures! Can you believe that?"

"Julia, you *must* try to be more tolerant, my dear! He *does* paint quite well. That copy of *The Honourable Mrs. Graham* is beautifully done."

"Paint indeed! Those colored photographs from the National Gallery and the British Museum! Those dreadful copies of Reynolds and Gainsborough! He once wanted to borrow my Zoffany."

Lady Thelma did not attempt to argue, knowing her friend's prejudices.

Mrs. Dodridge poured more coffee and went on.

"I said no. I told him that the insurance didn't cover the picture if it were removed from the house. I'm sure he thought I was lying, as indeed I was, but he had the grace to appear to believe me, and the matter dropped. Copy my Zoffany! What an idea!"

"Perhaps he thought Zoffany might be easier than Gainsborough."

"For a real artist it probably would, but it would have made no difference to *him*. He once tried to copy a Vermeer in the National Gallery. I saw the result. Thelma, for sheer technical and artistic incompetence, it was, in its own horrid way, an absolute jewel. Oh, dear!"

Lady Thelma lit a cigarette and looked at the smoke as she exhaled. Then she smiled, wanting to change the subject.

"Going back to the question of Cherton society, I'm not so sure that we don't really enjoy it here. After all, in retrospect, yesterday afternoon ought to be more amusing for you than annoying."

"My dear Thelma! Consider the dreadful boredom at the time! Am I—are we—to endure martyrdom nearly every day so we can eventually laugh at it? I like fun as well as the next person, but I prefer to achieve it through less taxing methods."

"I'll admit it can be rather dearly bought, Julia, but I'm fond of this part of the country, and, the inhabitants aside, this *is* a charming place to live. Do you know what young Jim Bradley told me? He's with BA, you know. He said that they had to stop using pictures of Cherton in BA advertisements because so many American insisted that the pictures must have been faked. They thought they were taken of cinema backgrounds.''

Mrs. Dodridge laughed.

''I'm not so sure they weren't. Sometimes I feel as if I were living in one of those interminable art films. The sort of thing Dostoevski might have written had he collaborated with Noël Coward.''

''If you mean that life in Cherton doesn't seem real, Julia, I can't agree. Certainly it lacks reality, but that's not at all the same thing. I suppose that if I were merely a tourist, it all might be mildly amusing, but to have to *live* with it, day in and day out—my God! Well, as you said, Why do we stay here?''

''Reality?'' Mrs. Dodridge shook her head. ''It depends on one's personal outlook, of course. It would be ghastly to have to spend an evening with Miss Bates in the flesh, but think how delightful she is in Jane Austen's hands.''

''Miss Bates is safely shut between the covers of a book. If we could lock up the Staines and the Hitchcocks in the library until we wanted to let them out, it would be—why, what's so amusing?''

Mrs. Dodridge was choking on her coffee.

''Don't! *Don't!* The idea of those four locked up together *anywhere* is delicious! Just consider the possible consequences!''

Lady Thelma grinned.

''Murder and suicide at the very least, I should think. Yes, the idea really has possibilities. Could we include his lordship, do you think?''

Mrs. Dodridge weighed the suggestion.

''I don't think it would accomplish anything. At least, anything constructive. Quite the reverse, probably. The Staines and the Hitchcocks would, I dare say, be so desperate among themselves that the introduction of a still-more-boring element in the person of Charlie Mauley would doubtless focus their concentrated despair on *him*—resulting in his immediate and probably painful demise."

Lady Thelma looked at her watch as she rose from her chair.

"If I didn't have to be in Porford by twelve, I should ask how you would propose to cope with Fanny Granby."

Mrs. Dodridge went with her friend to the door, and her eyes gleamed.

"I can tell you *exactly* what I should do with Fanny. I should shut her up in a cell with nothing but a copy of Fowler, and she shouldn't come out until she had read it at least three times."

Lady Thelma gazed reverently at Mrs. Dodridge.

"You know, Julia, Torquemada would have got on well with you."

As Mrs. Dodridge returned to the garden room, she sighed.

"But I wonder—still I really do wonder. Why *do* I stay in Cherton?" She grimaced. "Oh, *why* can't they make Frederick Staine the Bishop of Northwestern Australia?"

5

Miss Granby was at breakfast when the blond and astonishingly elegant Boudicca, her improbable and sole servant, brought the morning's letters. Boudicca was an excellent cook and an efficient housekeeper, but her name was one of the numerous burdens life had seen fit to lay upon Miss Granby's shoulders.

Boudicca's father, the harassed proprietor of the Rose Revived, had early in life developed an intense interest in and an extravagant admiration for the famous chieftainess. When, in due time, his conjugal exertions had produced a daughter, it was only natural that, in the teeth of the violent opposition of his wife, his mother, and his mother-in-law, his firstborn should be christened in honor of his heroine.

Boudicca Hoare was not particularly fond of her Christian name, and, in the common course of things, when she went into service, she would have been called by her surname in the usual way. It was not long before she realized why her several employers had chosen to address her as Boudicca. It is likely that she even derived some amusement from the situation.

Miss Granby was not the first to jib, but while her servant's given name was doubtless preferable to her unfortunate *nom de famille,* "Boudicca" was a violent irritant to Miss Granby's sense of humor, and she occasionally amused herself by wondering how her cook would look painted blue. She even went so far as to buy bright-blue uniforms, which the unsuspecting young woman wore until her exultant father saw her so dressed. Boudicca returned to her kitchen in a raging but respectful temper and firmly told Miss Granby that, if her services were to be retained, black uniforms would thereafter be de rigueur. Miss Granby had the good sense to apologize, and the wound healed. Boudicca's mistress tried to satisfy her own insatiable sense of the appropriate by planting woad in the kitchen window boxes. For the rest, she addressed her servant by name only when it was unavoidable.

The appearance of Boudicca with the post had aroused the foregoing thoughts, as her appearance usually did. Trying to shake her mind free of this bête noire (she impatiently repressed the suspicion of *bête bleue*), Miss Granby looked over her letters.

She scowled as she saw a thick envelope with *Encounter* printed on it. Another rejection, and one of her best pieces! She opened it viciously with her knife and then swore under her breath as she found the manuscript within smeared with currant jam and butter. Wiping the paper as best she could with her napkin, she unfolded the sheets. Attached to the first page was the nasty little rejection form she knew only too well. Her eye wandered over the opening lines. Really one of her better jobs, too! Editors were such fools! She savored the words:

The Psyche-Rejection
as a
Valid Entity

A Critical Evaluation
by
Frances P. Granby

It is not unlikely [she read] that at this point in time our conscious acceptance of the hypotheses advanced by (among others) Jean Genet, our not unwilling desire to conceive of *texture* as opposed to an extrapolated *concretivity,* our too easy if not rather superficial and not too really undesirable candour, our general tolerance of and exceptions to the materialistic conceptions of the folk-soul, will not serve to hinder our appreciation, our understanding, and our entirely too self-conscious evaluation of the *Weltansicht,* of the ethos, the proponents of which have hitherto, with a not unjustified *méchanceté. . . .*

Really, thought Miss Granby, really, it's too bad!

She did not doubt that her article was good. She had spent a month merely outlining the major points of her argument. She sighed and placed the manuscript in her lap. She looked through the remaining envelopes. A letter from her cousin in Hampshire. Another from that odd young man at Oxford who had set *Trivia* as a Handelesque cantata and wanted her to edit it. At the bottom of the pile was a large heavy envelope from the States.

Miss Granby had long intended to subscribe to *The Sewanee Review.* She had seen a copy many years before and had been fascinated by it. She was then a mere girl and had understood very little of what she read. She had always meant to order the magazine but only last December had she gotten around to doing so. Now, of course, with her experience in publishing—well, in writing, at least— she would, she was sure, find one or two useful ideas in this American quarterly. Indeed, she might send "The Psyche-Rejection" to them. She had once met a Mr. Leavis at a luncheon, and found that he had had articles published by the review. If he could, why not she? Why not, indeed?

Miss Granby gathered up her letters and went into the sitting room. It was a dark cold day, so she lit the gas fire, turned on the lamps, and drew the curtains. She settled herself comfortably on the sofa and began to read the first article in the Winter issue of *The Sewanee Review*. She had read no more than two lines when Boudicca called her to the telephone.

It was Mrs. Hitchcock, and she wanted Boudicca's recipe for strawberry fool.

"But it's March!" exclaimed Miss Granby.

"How really *clever*, my dear!" screamed the receiver. "I *do* so wish *I* had *your* quick wit!"

Miss Granby subdued a desire to howl into the mouthpiece.

"I mean," she explained, "that the recipe must be made with the fresh fruit. Frozen won't do, you know."

"I *do* know, my dear! I *know*! I do *so well* recall that, but I was *just* going through my cookery book, and I happened to think of it. And *then* I thought, No time like the present. . . . I always say that if there *is* something to be done, there's *no* time like the *present*!"

Mrs. Hitchcock's laugh ripped up its idiot octave.

Miss Granby longed to observe that the same could be said of dying—to ask, "*Is* that what you *always* say?"—but she refrained.

"I'll have Bou—, I'll have Cook write out the recipe and send it to you today," she promised.

"Oh, lovely, *lovely*! You *are* such a *dear*!"

Miss Granby cursed mentally and obscenely.

"What," came Mrs. Hitchcock's voice, "are you doing with yourself on this cold foggy *spring* morning?"

"Spring" was the cue for another ten seconds of the Hitchcock laugh.

Miss Granby was becoming desperate.

"I've been reading. The new *Sewanee Review* came today, and I'm never quite happy until I've given it my full attention."

There was a pause.

"The new—the new *what?*"

Miss Granby felt better.

"The new *Sewanee Review,*" she purred. "Of course you know it, I'm sure."

Another pause—a longer one.

"Oh. . . . Oh, of *course! The Swami Review?* Yes, I *adore* it! So *very* uplifting—if a *wee* little bit on the—ah—*mystic* side. But, my dear Fanny, I didn't realize that you're interested in Yoga."

Miss Granby's expression became fiendish.

"Not 'swami,' dear. 'Sewanee.' S-E-W-A-N-E-E." Thank heaven she had the thing in her hand! "It's a frightfully good quarterly published by an American university. It's a literary thing like—" (What was it like?) "—like *Encounter,* you know, or *Partisan.*"

The silence at the other end was tangible.

"I'm in the middle of a really fascinating article on Hopkins," Miss Granby went on happily. "I've always admired Hopkins, but I'd never realized how *much* there is to him. This present writer is really profoundly aware of Hopkins's more obscure implications. Perhaps you'd like to borrow it? It's *well* worth reading!"

In the hush following this shameless gambit, Miss Granby could almost hear the shreds of the Hitchcock ego trying to fit themselves together.

"It sounds—as you say, ah—fascinating. I must ask Thomas about the—what did you call it, dear?"

"*The Sewanee Review.* S-E-W—"

"Yes! Well, I shall do that. . . . And thank you *so* much, you clever, *reading* girl, for that fool recipe. Oh! That sounds so *rude,* doesn't it?"

The laugh rang out once more, and Mrs. Hitchcock rang off.

Miss Granby stood holding the receiver to her ear for a moment. Then she replaced the receiver and shook her head.

"Jesus Christ!" she muttered.

It was some time before Miss Granby could compose her mind to a really receptive literary mood. She asked Boudicca to make some coffee, and while she was waiting for it, she stumbled through the theme of "The Harmonious Blacksmith" on the spinet. When the coffee appeared, she went to the sofa and picked up the blue-bound magazine.

After twenty minutes, Miss Granby flipped back to the beginning of the article and began it again. After ten minutes, she began a third time, reading slowly and aloud. She was puzzled. She was also irritated. The author seemed to assume on the part of his reader a familiarity with Hopkins's poetry, a familiarity that Miss Granby was not within light-years of possessing. In fact, it must be said that she had never read a single line by Gerard Manley Hopkins. She had begun the article with the vague conviction that "Hopkins" was a hymnodist somehow connected with Sterndale Bennett. The lines quoted by the writer baffled her completely.

Miss Granby's studies in the States had been of a specialized nature, and although she knew rather more than she wanted to know about "psychology" of the variety affected by the lower middle class American "educators," her experience with and her exposure to the humanities were almost nonexistent. She had acquired a glib and facile jargon (although even *she* had drawn the line at "meaningful," "challenging," "culturally disadvantaged," and "peer group"), and she knew all the latest trends in writers, Beat and unBeat, but of her own country's literary wealth, she was startlingly ignorant. Milton, Pope, Fielding, Sterne, Austen, Scott, Byron, Browning, Dickens, Trollope, Hardy were merely names to her, and some, such as Edgeworth or Gaskell, were not even that.

This was not altogether her fault. Her father had been sent to Canada by his firm, and she was born in Ottawa. Circumstances eventually settled the Granbys in Wilmington, Delaware, and Fanny was sent to the University at Newark.

Neither better nor worse than many other state universities, Delaware gave Fanny what it could offer, which, bluntly speaking, was not much. After her graduation from the School of Education, she spent several years in "literary" circles in New York City. Because the members of her particular clique were as ignorant as she, she had no way of knowing what was really lacking. They read each other's poetry, discussed the obvious in tones of the most intense immediacy, and learned to believe that the proper label and the correct pigeonhole for every phase of human experience was the sure way to arrive at what they called an "understanding of life." That those labels and pigeonholes were utterly nonsensical, she had come only lately to suspect, although she should have realized that her sense of humor had tried to warn her.

Miss Granby was not stupid. She was undeniably a fake, but she had the merit of feeling ashamed of her posing. Only in Cherton could she have passed for an "intellectual." She could more than hold her own with people such as the Staines and the Hitchcocks, but she was uneasy and unhappy when thrown with Mrs. Dodridge, Lady Thelma, or Dr. Robbertson. That both women were the daughters of peers had no effect upon Miss Granby. She was not a snob in that sense, but she recognized their real superiority, and they made her ill at ease.

There were some genuine things about Miss Granby. She was kind, and, since her father's death had made it possible, she was generous with her comfortable income. She disliked gossip, and she held herself in contempt for her intimacy with the Staines and the Hitchcocks. She admired and respected Dr. Robbertson, although she thought she knew how profane and violent would be his reception of such sentiments. She liked him because he went his own way, being himself, and, she suspected, went out of his way to shock and mock the silly little world that was Cherton.

And so Miss Granby, curled up on the sofa before the gas fire, tried to understand what she was reading and wondered where she could borrow a copy of Hopkins's poems.

6

Lord Mauley removed his dressing gown and put one foot into the bath. Finding the temperature pleasant, he placed his other foot in the bath and lowered himself into the hot water, stretching out his legs and wiggling his toes as the warmth penetrated him. He wondered if he had put on weight: The water seemed to be unusually near the top of the tub. Or had Birkett run in more water than usual? But then Birkett never ran in too much water. Lord Mauley was sure of that because Birkett never made a mistake.

He looked down at his waist. It seemed fatter. Then he looked for the loofah. It was not on its rack. The soap was there, and a bottle of scented salts. Could he be sitting on the loofah? He squirmed slightly but could feel nothing beneath him except the smooth hot porcelain of the tub. He frowned. Then he squirmed again to be sure. The water splashed over the edge of the tub. Lord Mauley leaned back to allow the waves to subside, and as he did so, his eye caught sight of the loofah lying on the bath stool. Why should it be there? Had he put it there? Birkett wouldn't have put it there; he wasn't that sort of servant. The loofah was just out of reach, and Mauley wondered whether he could have his bath without it. He rose slowly and began to soap himself. No. He'd have to get the loofah, he thought. As he tried to soap his upper back, the cake flipped from his hand and came to rest near the bath stool. Lord Mauley stood for a moment looking at the soap. Then he looked at his hand as if another tablet of soap might possibly be in it. His hand was empty, so he grasped the cold-water tap for support and stepped out of the tub, reaching first for the loofah.

His hand came to rest upon the loofah at the precise second that his foot came to rest upon the soap. His grip tightened upon the tap, but that anchorage served only to transform a prosaic fall into a wild entrechat as Lord Mauley's bulk pivoted about the tap, overturning the bath stool and bringing him into violent and excruciating contact with the heavy steam-heated towel rack, which fell upon him as the chrome supports broke from the wall.

His attention momentarily devoted to screaming, Lord Mauley was unable to observe that the cold water was running full force, the tub overflowing to the floor upon which he lay pinned, an inverted version of St. Lawrence, beneath the bars of the towel rack. That he was merely grilled to medium rare by the rack instead of being drowned outright by the rising water, he owed to the arrival of Birkett, to whom the sound of a heavily falling body, the screams, and the wash of water into the passage had announced the beginning of another day at Mauley Hall.

As he lay thickly salved and dosed with a strong sedative, Lord Mauley meditated. A slight sound made him open his eyes. He saw Birkett beside the bed.

"The loofah was on the bath stool, Birkett," said Lord Mauley.

"Sir?"

"The loofah was on the bath stool, Birkett."

Birkett thought that this must have some significance. On the other hand, his employer's remark might be simply the result of shock or the herald of delirium. The doctor had mentioned both as likely reactions. (Birkett had wondered at the time how it would be possible to diagnose delirium in Lord Mauley.) He sighed.

"The loofah? Yes, sir."

Lord Mauley closed his eyes, and presently he was asleep.

"How is my brother?" asked the Hon. Mrs. Tunstall, who had arrived from London in response to a telephone call from the desperate Birkett.

The doctor, Sir Alistair Woodley, a cousin, replied that Charlie would be all right.

"But wasn't he dreadfully burned?" she asked.

"Oh, here and there," said Sir Alistair cheerfully, "but it won't bother him unless he sleeps on his stomach—and I shouldn't think he could do that anyway."

"But how did it *happen*? The bathroom looks as if a lorry'd been driven through it!"

"My dear woman, how does anything ever happen in this house? When I asked him, all *he* could say was that the loofah was on the bath stool."

"Well, why shouldn't it be?"

"*I* don't know. I don't know *anything*! Birkett says that when he got into the bathroom, Charlie was flat on his back in two inches of water and *under* the towel heater, which, for reasons best known to your brother, he seems to have removed from the wall."

"I—I suppose I'd better go up to see him?"

"Certainly—if you don't mind his being naked."

"Naked!" gasped Mrs. Tunstall. "Isn't he dressed yet?"

"No," said Sir Alistair, still more cheerfully, "and I doubt that he will be for some time. He can't bear even the weight of a sheet." He grinned. "Speaking of weight, the shock of this experience ought to wither away some of that blubber. Or *can* blubber wither? I must look it up—an interesting point, don't you think?"

"Alistair, you're perfectly heartless! *How* can you say such things?"

"It's necessary only to know Charlie. Then one can say anything. . . . And now, if you don't mind, Jean, I've other patients to see. They are, perhaps, a trifle less original in their afflictions than Charlie, but they have other compensations. . . . Remember, wear your dark spectacles when you visit your brother. He looks like a side of bacon painted by Turner. . . . By the way, I've given him a very strong sedative. But even if he's out like a light for the next eight hours, you'll still be able to read by him. Too bad he didn't *back* into the heater, speaking of Turner. We could've called him the *Lighting Derrière*."

"Nasty, unfeeling brute!" she muttered as her cousin drove from the door.

Mrs. Tunstall pondered. How long would she have to remain in this—this *trou*? Her whole weekend spoiled because Charlie couldn't have a bath quietly and without publicity! She rang for Birkett.

"See if you can reach my husband at his office, please. I'll come to the telephone if you can."

Then she sat down with a cigarette and a copy of *Queen*, trying to forget her brother, his bath, and his burns.

"Mr. Tunstall is on the line, ma'am," said Birkett.

"Jean, what is it? I'm on the verge of an important meeting. Do be brief, dear."

"Charlie is ill, Philip. I'm stuck here for God knows how long. I—I'm afraid you'll have to tell the Evanses that we can't have them tomorrow night."

"Oh, for God's sake! You know how important it is that I remain on good terms with Evans. What's the matter with Charlie? Is he seriously ill?"

"He—he was burned in the bath," said Mrs. Tunstall hopelessly.

There was a pause. Then her husband's voice came through with an edge.

"Burned in the *bath*? Are you trying to tell me he's boiled?"

"No, he was having a bath—and the heater—"

"Look, Jean! I've a string of clients outside and a directors' meeting in ten minutes. If your brother dies, let me know, and I'll come to the funeral. Otherwise I have more important things—and people—to think about!"

"Really, Philip! Charlie has a right to live, you know!"

"I deny it. I utterly deny it. I regard the mere fact of his existence as a personal and deliberate affront on the part of God Almighty. . . . Don't interrupt. I shall expect you for dinner tomorrow. If you're not here to meet the Evanses, you can just forget about that little trip to Cannes next month."

Gloomily, Mrs. Tunstall consulted Birkett.

"How is he?"

"Asleep, Mrs. Tunstall."

"Is—is there anything I can do, Birkett?"

"I can't think of anything, ma'am. Sir Alistair said that Lord Mauley would just have—have to lie there for a few days. Sister Benson is coming in to look after him. He—ah—he can't dress, you know, ma'am."

"Yes—so my cousin told me. . . . Does that wretched four-twenty still creep up to London?"

"Yes, ma'am."

"Very well. Have the car sent round for me at four. It's essential that I return to London at once. I'll be back in a few days. . . . I shall telephone my mother from London."

"I'll tell Lord Mauley when he awakens, ma'am."

"Perhaps—perhaps you might telephone the vicar later on in the afternoon. After I've left," she added hastily.

Birkett overcame the desire to close his eyes.

"I shall ring Mr. Staine as you suggest, Mrs. Tunstall. Perhaps Mr. Staine could have tea with Lord Mauley?"

"Yes—an excellent idea," she murmured vaguely. "Oh—there isn't an *earlier* train, is there?"

Of course there wasn't.

Lady Mauley crisply put down the telephone and glared at her maid.

"Tell Harkinson that if I hear those damned peacocks once more at half-past three in the morning, I'll not only shoot *them,* but I'll shoot *him*!"

"Yes, m'lady."

"And don't stand there gibbering as if you were tolerating a mental incompetent. I'm a good bit older than you, but although I may be infirm, I'm not senile! Tell Agnes I want to see her at once!"

"Yes, m'lady."

Brett, who was new to the job, fled the bedroom and descended to the ground floor. At the foot of the stairs, she encountered a chic woman of fifty.

"Miss Pollock, Lady Mauley would like to see you."

"Thank you, Brett. I'm just on my way up."

Miss Pollock, blond and regal, entered the bedroom to confront her aged cousin.

"Agnes! How many times must I request you not to come into my bedroom as if you were some sort of superior being? You're not!"

Miss Pollock smiled.

"What would you prefer?"

"I'd prefer that you get rid of that air of having just been awarded the Garter for inventing the wheel. You're really quite tiresome."

"Yes, Cousin Emily."

"In fact, you're very nearly as tiresome as that idiot son of mine. Do you know what he's done?"

"No, Cousin Emily."

"Of course you don't. And no one in her right mind could guess. With all your faults, you do have brains—of a sort."

"Yes, Cousin Emily."

"'Yes, Cousin Emily!'" snarled Lady Mauley. "Is that all you can say?"

"No, Cousin Emily."

"I'm delighted to hear it! . . . Well?"

"All right. What's Charlie done?"

"He's got himself burnt."

"Burnt?"

"*Stop* repeating everything I say, you goose! I said he was burnt!"

"Yes, Cousin Emily," said Miss Pollock maliciously.

Lady Mauley glowered. Then she smiled.

"Jean just telephoned me. Charlie has had an accident. It seems that he slipped in the bath and threw himself against the towel heater. I remember telling him that no one so large as he should have such a contrivance in so small a bath. It's a wonder he hasn't backed into it long since."

"He backed into the heater?" asked Miss Pollock.

Lady Mauley laughed shortly.

"No," she said, "he didn't back into it. Not that it matters."

Miss Pollock said nothing.

"I suppose I must go to Cherton. Horrible place. The daughter of Louis XV always referred to her duchy as *ce trou de Parme*. Well, that's how I feel about Cherton. But I shall have to go there. All those perfectly dreadful people. I shall *have* to do something about them! I may as well have *some* pleasure in the visit. God knows, there won't be much! Order the car, Agnes."

"Now?" asked Miss Pollock. It was a ninety-mile drive.

"Certainly. It's only eleven o'clock. I can easily be there for tea."

"But, Cousin Emily—"

"Don't argue! I know far better than you that I shall be ninety-five in July. What have I to worry about? If I die on the way, at least I shan't have to see Charlie. Ugh!"

"Well—are you ready to go?"

"I shall be by the time Smith discovers that there's no petrol in the car and that he's lost the maps. The old fool should have retired years ago. You remember the last time we drove to London, we arrived in Lympne?"

"All the more reason—"

"For God's sake, Agnes, stop arguing and order the car! I shall be ready before you are."

"You want *me* to go? I was going to Pelham Parva for lunch."

"Of course I want you to go! Do you think I'm going to trust myself alone to that lunatic? If we end up in Scotland, I want to have some kind of company—even yours."

"Very well, Cousin Emily."

"Tell Jerson to pack a lunch. And if she puts caviar-stuffed eggs in it, I shall discharge her. The last time she made up a lunch, I nearly died of thirst before we got to a pub. Now *go* order the car!"

"Yes, Cousin Emily."

"'Yes, Cousin Emily!'"

7

The Duchess of Devonshire stared glassily at Dr. Robbertson. Uneasily he stared back, wondering what was wrong. Then he picked up a small mirror and, turning his back to the duchess, carefully examined her reflection. He grunted. There was no doubt about it. The woman was cross-eyed. But which eye? He squinted and studied the reflection. Then he picked up the Medici print of the duchess and studied *it*. Sighing, he put down the print and picked up his palette knife. He was moodily scraping away the duchess's right eye when the doorbell rang.

"You answer it," muttered Dr. Robbertson, continuing to scrape. This was directed to his nephew, a young American of eighteen whose mother's recent death had left him the doctor's only surviving close relative.

"Like—like *this?*" asked the boy, who had been posing earlier and had not bothered to dress.

"Oh. Well, you'd better put on your bikini," said the doctor after surveying the auburn-haired youth lounging in the club chair.

The bell rang again.

"Do go on, Tommy," said his uncle. Damn Gainsborough anyway!

Reluctantly Tommy rose, pushed back his shoulder-length hair, and put on his brief nylon bikini. The doorbell rang a third time.

"My God! Haven't you gone yet? Please!"

"But—isn't there a robe or somethin'? My pants are upstairs," said the boy, looking himself over very dubiously.

Dr. Robbertson slammed down the palette knife.

"Oh, I'll go myself! Why didn't you dress sooner?"

As Dr. Robbertson left the room, Tommy returned to his chair, looking at the picture on the easel and at his own half-finished nude portrait leaning against the wall. His eye wandered back to the Duchess of Devonshire. Now half-blind, she seemed to be watching him. Annoyed, he peeled off his bikini, hoping that his uncle would bring whoever it was right on in. He stuck out his tongue at Her Grace. Christ! What a drag! Then Tommy cocked an ear toward the door.

"I hope you'll forgive my calling so unexpectedly, Doctor," said Miss Granby, "but I wondered if you happen to have a copy of Hopkins's poems."

Dr. Robbertson stared at his visitor.

"Gerard Manley Hopkins?" he asked, thinking how fresh and clear Miss Granby's skin looked.

"Er—yes," said Miss Granby a little nervously. That *was* his name, wasn't it?

"Why, yes. Please come in, and I'll look. I'm almost sure I know where to lay hands on it."

"Oh, thank you. It's very good of you," she said, walking into the hall.

"Why don't you just make yourself comfortable while I look? I shan't be a moment."

Miss Granby sat down as the doctor returned to his studio. Dr. Robbertson shut the door behind him and crossed to the bookcase, biting his lower lip in thought.

"Ah, here it is!" he murmured.

"What?" asked Tommy.

"A book Miss Granby wants to borrow." He looked at his nephew. "Don't you ever get cold, Tommy? If you don't mind, stay in here until she leaves, will you?"

"Okay, Robbie."

Miss Granby rose as the doctor returned.

"Am I interrupting you, Doctor?" she asked anxiously. "Should I come another time, perhaps?"

"No interruption at all. My young nephew from the States

has been posing for me—I wanted to be sure that he didn't come wandering in here in his wristwatch!"

Miss Granby smiled. Then her face became serious.

"I was sorry to hear of his losing his mother—your sister, wasn't she?" she asked sympathetically.

"Yes," said Dr. Robbertson. "You'll have to meet him when he's presentable. Perhaps you'll talk to him about the States. I'm afraid he's rather homesick, although—" The doctor left his thought unsaid.

"I should be glad to, Dr. Robbertson."

"Oh! Here's Father Hopkins. He was just where I thought he'd be, for a wonder," said the doctor.

"Thank you so much, Doctor. I'll take good care of it, I promise you."

"I'm sure you will. Keep it as long as you like, Miss Granby. I've another copy upstairs. I'm very fond of Hopkins."

"Are you? Perhaps—perhaps we could talk about his poetry one of these days? I really don't know it at all."

Dr. Robbertson smiled at her.

"I don't know that I'm much of an authority, Miss Granby, but if I can help you, I'll be happy to try."

With repeated thanks, Miss Granby left, and the doctor returned to his studio in a rather bemused frame of mind.

"This bloody eye!" muttered Dr. Robbertson, trying for the fourth time to place the iris correctly. Then he spoke over his shoulder to Tommy, who was lovingly combing his hair and looking contentedly at the result in the mirror.

"You're driving me bonkers, Tommy. I *do* wish you'd do *something* besides that! Why don't you read, or go for a walk, or have a bath?"

"I can't unnastan' th' books ya got," said Tommy, stretching his handsome self and yawning. "Ya don't have no sidewalks in this town, an' I'm not gonna ruin a sixty-buck pair of shoes in all that mud. Anyways, I'm tired. D'ya know whut time I got home this mornin'? Besides, I took a bath two hours ago."

"Oh, all right," said the artist, temporarily giving up on the duchess. "Do you want to go for a run in the car?"

"No—thanks."

"Well—"

Tommy looked contrite. "I'm sorry I'm so dumb, Robbie!"

"You're *not* dumb," said his uncle in an irritated tone. "You're just—you're just young. Would you like a drink?"

The doorbell rang, and Tommy reached for his bikini.

This time the doctor answered the summons at once. It was the vicar.

"Good *afternoon,* Doctor," said Mr. Staine, his tone implying that the Archbishop of Canterbury had just been lynched by drunken curates.

"I hope you'll not think me frightfully rude, Vicar," said Dr. Robbertson hurriedly, "but I'm extremely pressed at the moment. Would it be too much to ask you to let me call at the vicarage later this afternoon?"

"Ah—" Mr. Staine tried to sustain his expression, his mood, and his tone. The effort nearly overcame him. "Lord Mauley—is—" he began.

Dr. Robbertson cut in ruthlessly.

"Burned to a crisp, I hear. Frightful. However, my dear Vicar, I'm having a very important talk with my nephew—the poor young chap! I *know* you'll forgive me. About four at the vicarage?"

Before Mr. Staine could recover from the double shock of the doctor's reaction to Lord Mauley's tragic mishap and the flat refusal of a parishioner to admit the accredited representative of the Church, the door was shut, and Dr. Robbertson was pouring a drink for Tommy, who had pulled off his bikini again. The doctor shook his head as he poured, wondering whether he could get Tommy into a school of some sort. Borstal, perhaps?

8

Mrs. Hitchcock looked hopefully at her husband.

"Do you know *The—The Swanee Review?*" she asked.

Mr. Hitchcock thoughtfully clasped his hands beneath his chin.

"Why do you ask?" he replied.

Fanny Granby was expatiating upon its merits," said Mrs. Hitchcock.

"Mmm."

"What is it?" she asked.

"A review?" asked her husband.

"A literary quarterly—published by some American university, apparently."

"Ah, yes! Of course!" said Mr. Hitchcock knowingly.

"You do know it, then?" asked his wife.

"No."

"Fanny Granby does," she said.

One less preoccupied with himself might have said, "Jolly good for Fanny!" Thomas Hitchcock said nothing.

"Fanny said that there was an interesting article about Hopkins."

"Hopkins? The psalm man?" asked Mr. Hitchcock.

"Psalms?"

"Wrote 'em with Sternhold—sixteenth century or thereabouts."

"I dare say," said his wife. Then she added cautiously, "Is there any *other* Hopkins?"

Mr. Hitchcock ruminated pontifically.

"Wasn't there a priest chap—end of the century—who wrote some sort of drivel? Poems? Peacocks and things rushing about a dark room?"

"Peacocks in a dark room, Thomas?"

"Well, it was something like that. That's all I remember. Old Sturridge was great on Hopkins and his blessed peacocks."

"I'm sure I don't know," said Mrs. Hitchcock helplessly. "Oh! Those roses are shedding! I *knew* I'd cut them too late!"

"Manure," remarked Mr. Hitchcock.

"What?"

"Need more guano—lots of it. Keep 'em healthy and thriving."

"Oh."

Félicité Dupont, a displaced Frenchwoman employed by the Hitchcocks, entered.

"Mr. Staine, Madame."

Mrs. Hitchcock leaped to her feet, and her husband clambered out of his chair.

As the vicar began to preside over the drawing room, Félicité returned to the kitchen.

The rear bell rang. It was Boudicca.

"Good day, Miss Hoare," said Félicité.

Afternoon," said Boudicca. She held out a slip of paper. "Here's the recipe for the fool."

"Comment?" asked Félicité, taking the paper.

"It's for Mrs. Hitchcock," said Boudicca. "Miss Granby asked me to bring it over." She frowned. "It's March."

Félicité's command of English was uncertain, and she was not sure that she had heard Boudicca correctly.

"What fool?" she asked.

"Strawberry," replied Boudicca. "Good-bye." And she took herself off down the kitchen walk to the back gate.

Félicité shook her head and returned to the drawing room.

The vicar had just concluded his account of his visit to Mauley Hall.

"How *dreadful*!" exclaimed Mrs. Hitchcock.

"Frightful!" agreed her husband.

"Madame?"

"Oh—yes? What is it, Félicité?"

"Miss Granby sent this to the fool," said Félicité, looking first at her mistress and then at her master. Could it be for the *curé*? (Mr. Staine was looking startled.)

Puzzled, Mrs. Hitchcock took the paper and unfolded it. Then she laughed. Félicité winced in spite of herself, but no one noticed.

"How amusing! Thank you, Félicité! It's for me—*pour le pouding, comprenez?*"

"Oui, madame," said Félicité, baffled. *"Pour le pouding."*

She left the room with the air of Andromaque going off to consult Hector's tomb. *Mon Dieu! Les Anglais!*

Mrs. Hitchcock turned brightly to the vicar.

"Françoise vient d'm'envoyer une recette—c'est un pouding exquise!"

"Exquis," muttered Mr. Hitchcock.

"Oh, how *silly* of me! *Do* forgive me, Vicar! After rattling away to poor Félicité, I seem to forget that I'm talking French!"

Thomas Hitchcock repressed the observation that she wasn't. Then he returned to the vicar's news. The whole village, of course, had been babbling about it since one of the Hall housemaids, wild-eyed with delight, had related it to her cronies shortly before noon. Still, Thomas Hitchcock knew what was due the cloth.

"Poor, poor man," he said in a hushed voice.

Mr. Staine nodded. "He can't dress, you know," he said in the tone he usually reserved for the consecration of the Elements.

"How *dreadful*!" exclaimed Mrs. Hitchcock.

"Frightful!" agreed her husband.

"I—I thought perhaps—if you had a few roses in your greenhouses to spare—?" said the vicar tentatively.

"Of *course*! I'll cut some at once, and Thomas can take them over."

"With—ah, perhaps one of your charming little notes, dear Mrs. Hitchcock? You write such *charming* little notes!"

"Oh, Vicar! You wily, *wily* man! You know *just* how to wrap me around your little finger!"

The vicar smiled suavely and rose to leave.

"I was sure you'd be anxious to try to cheer Lord Mauley. Unfortunately, not—ah—*all* of our friends are quite so—but I shouldn't cast stones. 'Let him who is—ah—without—'umm! Well, everyone has their limitations, of course."

"So few know them," murmured Mr. Hitchcock.

"Umm? Oh, yes—to be sure. 'To know thyself' is *not* given to all, is it? Well, *good*-bye. Time presses, I find, and I must call upon Lady Thelma before I return to the vicarage."

The Hitchcocks, like a destroyer escort, saw the vicar to the front door. As the door closed, Mr. Hitchcock frowned thoughtfully.

"Hopkins was an R.C.," he said.

His wife looked perplexed.

"Who?"

"That poet chap."

Mrs. Hitchcock's mind was even more of a blank than usual.

"What poet chap?" she asked listlessly.

"You know, Portia. Peacocks rushing about."

"Rush about. I thought peacocks were sedate and pompous."

Mr. Hitchcock frowned more deeply.

"You never can tell what an R.C. will make of an idea. There was all that trouble with Henry VIII, you know."

"Oh! I *must* get those flowers!"

"Do," said Mr. Hitchcock.

"How *fortunate* that you mentioned the War of the Roses!"

"I didn't," he said.

His wife was already out of hearing.

"Manure," he remarked.

9

Lady Thelma Mullen replaced the telephone on its cradle and snorted. Then she picked up the instrument again and dialed.

"May I speak to Mrs. Dodridge, please, Edwards?"

As she waited, she drew knives and hatchets on the pad on the table.

"Hello, Thelma. What's on your mind?"

"That—that unspeakable Hitchcock woman just rang me. You'd never guess what she wanted."

"All right, I shan't try."

"She actually asked me if I would take some flowers up to the Hall—for Charlie Mauley!"

"Well, that *was* thoughtful of her! Have her blessed gardeners gone on strike?"

"That's just what *I* wanted to ask. I *did* ask her where she thinks I'm going to find flowers in *my* garden. The only green thing in the place is that bronze Priapus. *Then* she laughed. By the time my hearing returned, I could just make out something about my telephoning the florist at Porford. Can you imagine that?"

"Knowing Dracula's Daughter, yes. I'm surprised she didn't suggest that you drive up to town for them."

"I told her very politely that I would do what I could, and while she was telling me how kind I am, I rang off before she could laugh again."

"What *are* you going to do, Thelma?"

"Oh, I'll have Dobbins make a jelly or something nourishing."

"You'd better keep an eye on Dobbins, Thelma. As Birkett's sister, she might put rat poison in it."

"If I thought Dobbins capable of that, I'd send a gracious gift to Portia Hitchcock—a sort of thank-you for her little hint."

"Thelma, what *is* the matter with Charlie Mauley? I've heard all sorts of tales today."

"So've I. According to Robbie, whom I met in the village this morning, Charlie fell out of the bath and onto the towel heater. Apparently he's burned rather nastily."

Mrs. Dodridge clicked her tongue. "Too bad," she said. "I hope he's not seriously hurt."

"I don't think so. Robbie said—*oh, my God*!"

"What's the matter?"

"The vicar! He's coming through the gate. I'll have to ring you back."

Mr. Staine seated himself and eyed Lady Thelma with an expression that she assumed was intended to convey pitying compassion.

"I dare say you've heard of Lord Mauley's unfortunate accident?"

Lady Thelma contrived to arrange her features in a properly solemn expression, but she did not trust herself to speak, and so only nodded.

"*Most* regrettable." The vicar sighed.

Lady Thelma felt that she must say something, but her mind was empty. At least it was devoid of any remark that she could suitably make to Mr. Staine. She nodded again and repeated his comment.

"I saw him," continued the vicar. "A piteous sight, I assure you, my dear Lady Thelma. Burned. Badly, badly burned."

"Where?" asked Lady Thelma, unable to check herself.

The vicar chastely lowered his eyes to the carpet.

"Ah—chiefly between his—lower, ah, abdomen and his—um, upper thighs."

Lady Thelma lowered her own eyes and put her hand to her mouth to conceal her expression.

"Dreadful! Simply dreadful!" said Mr. Staine mournfully.

"How—how did it—happen?" she asked—with difficulty.

"A fall, I believe. A fall in the bath."

"Did he break any bones?"

The vicar shook his head.

"No. *That* was a blessing indeed. Such falls can be very dangerous."

"Yes," agreed his hostess. "They can indeed. Very dangerous." She wondered how much longer the interview would last. "Have you seen Julia Dodridge?"

"Not yet. I shall go there from here. I stopped by the Hitchcocks' on my way here. I thought that I should call upon those who make up our little circle. *Dear* Mrs. Hitchcock is sending Lord Mauley some flowers, I believe. *So* considerate of her!"

"Yes," said Lady Thelma frantically. "So few people would have thought of it."

"Ah, yes. True! True! We are not *all* so thoughtful, I sometimes fear." Mr. Staine shook his head gravely; then he cleared his throat. "Now, *you,* of course—"

Lady Thelma's eyes began to glitter. However, she merely said, "I thought that I might send Lord Mauley a delicate little wine jelly—one of Dobbins's favorite puddings."

"Very, *very* thoughtful of you," said Mr. Staine, nodding with grave approval. "Very, *very* thoughtful."

"In fact," she said, in calm desperation, "I was just about to tell Dobbins when you arrived. You say you've not seen Julia?"

Surprisingly, the vicar took the hint and rose.

"No, and I must run along. Thank you, Lady Thelma. I'm sure Lord Mauley will be *most* grateful to you for your kind sympathy in this—ah, time of *trial.*"

Lady Thelma saw him to the door. As it closed behind him, she dived for the telephone.

"Julia!"

"Has he gone?"

"Yes, I've just disincumbented myself—but he's on the way to *your* house now!"

"I suppose you suggested it, you beast. Well, thanks for the warning. The Dolmetsch man is here. I'll tell him to make plenty of noise. Oh, Thelma? Will you ring me at five-minute intervals?"

"With pleasure. But please warn Edwards so she won't think I've gone mad."

"I'll just tell her that you'll be ringing frequently—and not to announce who's calling," said Mrs. Dodridge.

Lady Thelma wished her friend luck and braced herself to order the wine jelly.

10

Edwards, her face a study in controlled composure, ushered Mr. Staine into Mrs. Dodridge's drawing room. The vicar was surprised to see a strange man in shirt-sleeves bending over the harpsichord at the far end of the room. The man's jacket was on a chair, and bits of cloth, wire, and felt were strewn about the floor, together with parts of the instrument.

Mrs. Dodridge went forward to welcome her guest.

"Mr. Staine! What a pleasant surprise! You must forgive the clutter. Mr. Bone has come from Dolmetsch's. He has to make some adjustments in the harpsichord. I do hope you won't mind if we sit in here? Mr. Bone always has a *thousand* questions to ask me as he works."

"Oh—ah, quite so. From Dolmetsch's, is he?"

"Yes—all the way from Surrey—so you see, I really have to take advantage of his visit. Do sit down and—"

The rest of her words were inaudible as Mr. Bone began to play clashing chords from one end of the keyboard to the other.

The vicar sat down.

"I—I suppose you've heard of Lord Mauley's—"

"What did you say, Vicar?"

Mr. Staine raised his voice. *"I said, I suppose you've heard of Lord Mauley's—"*

The noise suddenly stopped, and the vicar found that he was shouting. "—Lord Mauley's unfortunate accident," he continued, reducing his volume.

"Ooooh, yes," said Mrs. Dodridge, nodding sympathetically. "I was really quite shocked to—yes, Edwards?"

"There's—I think it's a trunk call, ma'am. Do you wish to take it?"

"A trunk call? Oh, yes. Please excuse me, Vicar. I'll be—"

Her words were drowned as Mr. Bone began again. The vicar heard only noise, but Mrs. Dodridge recognized it as the opening movement of Bach's *Italian* Concerto. Mr. Bone played by ear, and she was glad to flee.

Surreptitiously, Mr. Staine looked at his watch. Then he looked at Mr. Bone, a short man with a surprisingly long black beard. The vicar wondered whether it ever got tangled in the strings. He sighed as the music stopped abruptly and Mr. Bone began to hit one key repeatedly. It was a very high note, and after fifty seconds, the vicar wondered whether he was going mad.

Mrs. Dodridge reappeared and smiled apologetically.

"So confusing. I'm terribly sorry, Vicar. Now let's have a comfortable chat. You were talking about Lord Mauley. Such a frightful mishap."

"Indeed it was," said Mr. Staine. "I'm afraid that he'll be laid up for quite some time."

"I'm most distressed to hear that. Oh, excuse me. Yes, Mr. Bone?"

"It's the upper eight-foot that's giving the trouble, is it, Mrs. Dodridge?"

"Well," said Mrs. Dodridge, rising and going toward the instrument, "well, actually, it's the lute jacks brushing against the upper eight."

"Hmmm," said Mr. Bone. He moved a stop knob and played a chord. "Needs a bit of regulation, that slide. I'll see what I can do, Mrs. Dodridge. Not a very difficult job, this one."

Mrs. Dodridge returned to her chair by the vicar.

"So Lord Mauley will be in bed for a while, you think?"

"I'm afraid so. I thought that perhaps you . . ." he paused as Edwards came in.

"Beg pardon, ma'am, but His Grace is on the line."

"Oh, dear," said Mrs. Dodridge. "My brother is in hospital in Glasgow. I do hope nothing has gone wrong. I shan't be long, Vicar."

Mr. Staine smiled uncertainly and nodded. As Mrs. Dodridge left, a wildly unorthodox version of "For All the Saints" crashed from the instrument. Mr. Staine sat and endured, but beneath the protection of the harpsichord, he uttered some extremely unclerical expletives. The hymn climbed to a riotous finale as Mrs. Dodridge returned.

"Nothing seriously wrong, I trust?" asked Mr. Staine.

"Wrong?" asked Mrs. Dodridge, puzzled. Then she recollected. "Oh, *wrong*! No, indeed. My—brother had some questions about family matters. I really don't know why he didn't write. He quite startled me."

"Mrs. Dodridge?" said Mr. Bone.

"Yes?"

"Would you take a look at this, please?"

Mrs. Dodridge gave the vicar a smile and went again to the harpsichord. Mr. Bone pointed to something.

"Your belly's too rigid," he said.

In spite of years of training, Mr. Staine's eyes bulged.

"Is it really?" asked Mrs. Dodridge anxiously.

"You're warped, Mrs. Dodridge," continued Mr. Bone, "and when you're warped, Mrs. Dodridge," continued Mr. Bone, "and when you're warped like that, your belly gets stiff."

"Oh, dear! Is it serious, Mr. Bone?"

"Can't tell yet. May have to have it in the shop. Nasty bit of work that. Lot of talk about the fine old craftsmen. Lot of rot. Cut and chop, cut and chop—that's the way they put 'em together. Well, I'll get it into some sort of order, but I'm worried about your belly. I'll talk to the chief, but I think he'll tell you to send it to us for a proper job."

"Oh, dear," said Mrs. Dodridge again. "Sometimes I think it would be better just to sell—oh, Mr. Staine, must you be going?"

"Yes—yes. I—I find it's later than I thought. Lela will be wondering what's become of me."

They were going out of the door when Edwards came forward.

"Excuse me, ma'am, but Melbourne, Australia's calling."

The vicar, who had been about to suggest that one of his hostess's books on Dresden china would temper Lord Mauley's suffering, found himself deserted with yet another apologetic smile, and he was led by the sedate Edwards to the front door. There was really nothing left for him to do but to walk through it. As he went down the path, he was puzzled to hear faint but unmistakable screams of maniacal laughter through an almost frightening rendition of the "Anvil Chorus."

11

Miss Granby had just completed her thirty-third reading of "The Windhover," and was thinking of having a go at *The Peterkin Papers* as a welcome change, when the doorbell rang. It was Boudicca's afternoon out, so Miss Granby answered the summons. She peered through the blind and winced. Then she opened the door.

"Lela, dear! How lovely to see you!" she exclaimed.

Lela Staine came in, brushing the globules of condensation from her raincoat.

"Frightful day! Terribly damp, Fanny."

"Yes, I suppose it is. A typical March afternoon," replied Miss Granby.

"Oh, yes. March. It's lovely, really. One of my favorite months. I *really* do like it, you know!"

"March?"

"Oh, yes. I'm very fond of March. Especially at this time of the year," said Mrs. Staine, shrugging off her coat. "Oh, thank you. Just put it anywhere, dear."

"Come into the sitting room. It's quite pleasant with the fire going."

"Oh, you extravagant thing! That's your American sojourn coming out, isn't it?"

"Possibly," said Miss Granby, "but gooseflesh was coming out until I lit the fire. This house is dreadfully damp."

"Oh, my dear! You *know* what that wretched vicarage is like! Just one endless round of mold and mildew! Frederick's boots are perfect martyrs to it!"

Mrs. Staine sat down before the heat and toasted herself comfortably. Miss Granby seated herself in an armchair at an angle to the sofa and waited for some explanation of the unexpected call. Perhaps Mrs. Staine sensed this.

"I thought I ought to talk to you about Lord Mauley," she said.

"Lord Mauley?" asked Miss Granby.

"Yes. Wouldn't you like to do something?"

Miss Granby, not having heard the dreadful news, was puzzled.

"Do something?" she asked.

"As a gesture," explained Mrs. Staine unhelpfully.

"I—I'm afraid I don't quite understand. What sort of gesture?"

Mrs. Staine raised her eyebrows and joined the palms of her hands, her fingertips touching. The effect was that of a startled Virgin.

"Don't you *know*?" she asked in a low voice.

"Know?" repeated Miss Granby. "Is—is something wrong with Lord Mauley?"

"Oh, my *dear*! You mean you've not *heard*?"

It would be inaccurate to say that Mrs. Staine licked her chops, but the effect was much as if she had.

"Is—is he dead?" asked Miss Granby. No lesser disaster seemed probable, judging from Mrs. Staine's manner.

"*Dead*! Oh, *no*! But so *dreadfully* burned."

Miss Granby was at sea. She had spent most of the day trying to cope with Hopkins, and Boudicca was not the sort of servant who gossips with her employer.

"Burned?" she asked. "How?"

"In the bath," said Mrs. Staine.

"In the *bath*?"

"Yes, dear. That stupid man of his ran in too much hot water, and poor Lord Mauley accidentally fell into the bath. Scalded! Simply scalded!"

Do what she would, Miss Granby could not prevent there arising in her mind the vision of a lobster-red peer screaming in his bath. With an effort, she composed her features and clicked her tongue.

"I *knew* you'd be disturbed," cooed Mrs. Staine. "*So* shocking! I understand that Mrs. Tunstall came down immediately."

"Does—does Lady Mauley know?" asked Miss Granby, unable to think of anything else to say.

"Oooh, I doubt it. After all, she's—what—ninety-five?"

Miss Granby was dubious. She considered Lady Mauley one of the few sensible members of that noble family.

"Well, I'm quite sorry to hear this," said Miss Granby. "Can he—can Lord Mauley have visitors?"

"Oh!—My *dear*! The poor man! He was burned so badly that he can't dress. Can't have even a sheet over him!" Mrs. Staine lowered her voice to a pitch of incriminating confidence. "My dear Fanny—his—ah—um—*personal*—ah, *attachments* were almost *seared*! Um—Frederick saw him."

Miss Granby swallowed and then choked. When she had recovered, she stared at Mrs. Staine, trying vainly to think of something to say that would not damn her forever in Cherton.

"Dreadful!" she finally muttered.

"Dreadful!" agreed Mrs. Staine.

"Is—is the vicar going to see him tomorrow?" asked Miss Granby.

"Oh, *yes*! He's able to see Lord Mauley as often as possible."

"Perhaps he could take Lord Mauley something to read. You know. Something to take his mind off his—misfortune."

"How *very* kind of you! But then nearly everyone is so kind!"

"Nearly?" asked Miss Granby curiously.

"Well, my dear Fanny," said Mrs. Staine with a stained-glass expression, "we are not *all* able to share in the misfortunes of others, you know. Dr. Robbertson was, I fear, rather—ah—*callous* in his attitude."

"Really?"

"Oh, yes. A strange man, you know. Very, *very* strange."

It was Miss Granby's opinion that the doctor was one of the least strange persons in Cherton, so she said nothing.

"Suffice to say, Fanny, that he *refused, actually refused*, to allow Frederick to enter his house this afternoon! Almost laughed at poor Lord Mauley's unfortunate accident. Really, one never knows *when* one is going to be shocked next!"

"Perhaps," said Miss Granby doubtfully, wishing that she could talk to the doctor without restraint.

Mrs. Staine dropped her voice to such a pitch that the gas fire competed with her next remark.

"Frederick said that Dr. Robbertson quite brazenly told him that he was, ah, *occupied*—whatever *that* meant!—with his so-called 'nephew!'"

Mrs. Staine drew back and eyed Fanny knowingly, her head nodding and her lips pursed.

"He's an extremely attractive boy," said Miss Granby, who had never laid eyes on him but was fed up. "I should like to paint him myself." And not blue, either, she thought.

Mrs. Staine's eyes opened wide.

"Oh, my *dear* Fanny! You *can't* be serious!"

"Well," replied Miss Granby, discretion reminding her that she had to live in Cherton, "maybe not, but I do think there's rather too much talk and unfounded gossip about Dr. Robbertson. I think it's only Christian to try and be understanding." What utter drivel I'm talking!

"Oh, of course! Of *course*! One should *always* be a Christian! I mean, *where* should we be if we *weren't*?"

I've very often wondered, Miss Granby thought grimly, but all she said was, "I think so. . . . Well, perhaps I could ask the vicar to take a book or two up to Lord Mauley. And I've some very good pears that I've just had sent down from Fortnum's. Do you think he'd like those?"

"My dear Fanny! How *thoughtful*! Of course! I'm sure the poor man would be *delighted*!"

"Well, if Mr. Staine can stop by tomorrow morning on his way to the Hall, I'll have everything ready."

"Thank you, Fanny. Well—I must trot back to the vicarage. I've *dozens* of pots of jam to seal before tea. *So* nice to have had this little chat. *Good*-bye!"

Miss Granby saw Mrs. Staine to the door. Then she went to the telephone.

"Hullo?" said a young male voice.

"Uh—is Dr. Robbertson there, please? This is Frances Granby calling."

"Oh. Jussa minute."

Miss Granby could hear "A lady wants ya, Robbie"; then

a hand was obviously clamped over the mouthpiece at the other end. After a pause: "Miss Granby?"

"Dr. Robbertson, I hope I've not disturbed you, but Lela Staine was just here—about Lord Mauley."

"Oh, yes. He's burned."

"But is he really ill? I couldn't be sure."

"I don't think so. Mrs. Tunstall came down, I'm told, and then went right back to London. Mrs. Dodridge just called me, and I understand that there's more shock than damage. He can eat, of course, so I'm going to ask Tommy to make some fudge for the old boy and take it over tomorrow."

"Does your nephew cook, then?"

"Only fudge, but he does it quite well—and Lord Mauley, you know, has a sweet tooth."

"Yes. Well, do you know what really happened to him?"

"Evidently he slipped in the bath and whanged up against the towel rack. I dare say he'll be up in a few days. I've got to see Sir Alistair in a few minutes, and I can probably find out something from him."

"Well, I'd like to know," said Miss Granby carefully. "I mean, I don't want to appear indifferent if he's really ill, but I can't see becoming hysterical." She weighed her next remark. "I don't suppose he dented his coronet?"

Dr. Robbertson burst into laughter.

"Good for you! Frankly, Miss Granby, I hadn't expected that of you!"

"Well, *you* know what Cherton is like, Dr. Robbertson."

"Do I not! Look, I say, why don't you come over for tea this afternoon?"

"Why—why, I'd be very glad to, if it's convenient."

"Of course it's convenient. Shouldn't ask you if it weren't. About half-past four?"

Oh, lovely. I'll be there on the dot."

"You—you won't mind if Tommy's here?"

"Certainly not. I should like to meet him. And perhaps you can explain what on earth this dear Hopkins man is trying to say."

Dr. Robbertson had momentarily forgotten Hopkins, but he rallied manfully.

"I'll do my best, Miss Granby. See you at half-past four!"

Miss Granby hung up the telephone and smiled to herself.

Lady Mauley gave a little scream and rapped with her stick on the dividing window as she reached for the speaking tube.

"There's the turn! . . . And he's going past it! Smith! *Smith!* Stop! That's the turn for Cherton!"

"I see it, mum," mumbled the myopic Smith through the speaking tube.

"But you *don't* see it! You've just gone past it! *Oh*—"

"Now, Cousin Emily—"

"Do be quiet, Agnes! *Smith!* Stop the car and turn it around!"

The Daimler continued to creep along as Smith peered over his shoulder at the vanishing intersection.

"Smith! Are you mad, man? *Stop the car!*"

Smith placed his foot on the brake pedal and then fumbled for the ignition switch. The car stopped. Smith shook his head, pushed back his cap, and sighed. Then he turned to gaze blearily at his empurpled employer.

"You—you wants me to turn around, mum?" he asked.

Lady Mauley drew in her breath sharply and compressed her lips. She closed her eyes and slowly nodded.

Miss Pollock, torn between wishing to shake Smith and to laugh at her cousin, pointed back at the desired road.

"That road," she said, "is the way to Cherton. We have to take it if we're going to Cherton, you know, Smith."

Smith nodded comprehendingly and started the car. Since the main road was a narrow one, he decided to back to the intersection, depending upon what he saw in front of him to guide him to what he could not see behind him.

There was a bone-shattering jar, and the car tilted crazily into a culvert.

Now nearly reclining at a thirty-degree angle, Lady

Mauley folded her hands in her lap and smiled sweetly at her companion.

"I shall sit here, Agnes," she said.

Miss Pollock was peering out of the window.

"I don't think you will for long, Cousin Emily. We're in a ditch full of water that's well over the boot. If we sink any more, the water will come in the windows."

"I was a fool to have come," said Lady Mauley matter of factly.

"Yes, Cousin Emily," said Miss Pollock, with conviction. The old woman glared at her and burst into laughter.

"Where's the rest of that lunch, Agnes?"

Miss Pollock looked at Lady Mauley with satisfaction and replied, "In the boot."

Smith had not moved since the catastrophe. The car was tilted so that the front seat was considerably higher than the rear one. It seemed more than probable that the front wheels were in the air.

"Smith?"

"Yes, mum?"

"What are you going to do now?"

"Don't rightly know, mum. Can't get out. The door's jammed up against that there rock."

"Try the other door, Smith," suggested Miss Pollock.

"That's the one the lock doesn't work on. Can't open it *ever*."

Miss Pollock looked at Lady Mauley.

"It does seem to me, Cousin Emily, that with your income you could manage to—"

"Oh, be quiet, Agnes! I'm thinking!"

"Very well, Cousin Emily. I shall have a nap."

"You'll have nothing of the sort! You're going to help me out of this idiotic machine, and then we'll try to find a farmhouse with a telephone."

"What about Smith? He *can't* get out."

"He got us in. Let *him* worry about drowning! Now—can we get out on your side?"

"I think so. There seems to be a bit of stonework we can walk on."

"All right. Help me up. There—take my stick. Oh, *damn* Smith!"

There was no farmhouse. Lady Mauley and Miss Pollock trudged on through the encircling gloom. Suddenly, there was the sound of an engine.

"Is that a motorcar?" asked Lady Mauley.

"It sounds more like a motorbicycle," replied Miss Pollock, straining her eyes.

There came into view an ancient Vespa with a single rider. Lady Mauley waved her stick frantically, and the cyclist came to a halt a little beyond them. He was a young man of about twenty, with thick curly black hair and a leather jacket. He smiled ingratiatingly at the two women.

"What's the trouble, ladies?" he asked.

"We've had a motor accident," said Miss Pollock. "We'd like to ring a garage for help—only there doesn't seem to be a telephone about here."

"No," said the young man, "there isn't."

Miss Pollock and Lady Mauley exchanged glances.

The young man grinned.

"I'm going to Cherton," he said. "I can tell them to send someone from the garage, if you want me to."

"To *Cherton*?" asked Lady Mauley, eyeing the Vespa cautiously.

"*Now,* Cousin Emily!"

"Be quiet, Agnes! . . . Young man, may I ask your name?"

The cyclist grinned more broadly.

"Sure. I'm Dirk Henderson. . . . Who're you?"

"I'm Lady Mauley—my son lives at Cherton," she said.

"*Really,* Cousin Emily!" muttered Miss Pollock.

"Oh! You live at Maulcaster House, ma'am?" he asked.

"More or less," said Lady Mauley, smiling.

"I live at Pelham Parva, ma'am. Guess we're neighbors."

"Neighbors!" muttered Miss Pollock.

"Be *quiet,* Agnes!"

The young man laughed.

"I like you, ma'am!" he exclaimed.

"Thank you, Mr. Henderson," said Lady Mauley. "Do you think you might give me a—ah, *lift* in on that contrivance?"

He stared at her in consternation.

"But—but, ma'am—"

Lady Mauley raised her eyes to the overcast heavens.

"How dreadful it is when people think that because one is old, one has no sense of adventure!" she exclaimed.

"My God!" murmured Miss Pollock.

Dirk Henderson looked from one woman to the other. Then he patted the rear seat affectionately.

"It's not bad, ma'am, if you hang on tight—to me." He gave Lady Mauley a friendly wink.

"It's been a long time since a pretty young man was so cordial," said Lady Mauley, admiring his teeth. Then she handed him her stick and hitched up her skirts. Before Miss Pollock's unbelieving gaze, Lady Mauley seated herself astride the Vespa.

"As soon as I get to Cherton, Agnes, I shall have them send the car for you and Smith," she said composedly.

"We're only eight miles from Cherton," said the youth. "Sorry I can't take you both."

Miss Pollock was still openmouthed as Henderson and Lady Mauley disappeared over the hill.

12

Although Alfred Birkett was ostensibly Lord Mauley's butler, circumstances were such that he was also auxiliary valet and, on occasion, Lord Mauley's secretary. As Birkett stood at the Hall door, wondering when the thick mist would lift, he heard the sputtering approach of a motorbicycle.

Through the murk, there were barely discernible a young man on a Vespa and a heavily muffled figure sitting behind him. The Vespa came to a grinding stop on the gravel sweep before the entrance, and the young man looked back at his passenger.

"Is this the place, ma'am?" he asked.

The figure nodded and began to dismount. Its face was swathed in a woolen scarf.

"Here, here! What's going on, you chap?" called Birkett. "You don't want to come in here! This is a private drive! Can't you see that?"

The voice that came from the swathings of the scarf petrified Birkett.

"Don't be a fool, Birkett! Come here and help me off this insane vehicle!"

Birkett, incredulous, stood frozen on the steps.

"La—Lady *Mauley*?" he asked in stupefaction.

"Do you think I'm Lady Godiva? Come *help* me, Birkett!"

With the assistance of Birkett and Dirk, Lady Mauley disentangled her legs and stood upright. Then she turned to Dirk.

"A remarkable experience, Mr. Henderson. I had—no *idea*—"

"Are you all right, ma'am?" he asked anxiously.

"Of course I'm all right! What a magnificent device for the liver! Is tea ready, Birkett?"

"Yes, Lady Mauley," replied Birkett weakly.

"Splendid! Come in, Mr. Henderson. You need a cup of tea, I'm sure."

"Oh—I—I don't think I'd better, ma'am. My clothes . . ." the young man trailed off in an embarrassed manner.

"Your clothes are perfectly presentable, Mr. Henderson," said Lady Mauley firmly, and she shepherded him and Birkett ahead of her. The three mounted the steps, Dirk uneasy, awed by what he saw. The Hall was the sort of place he had always had to pay fifty pence to visit as a tripper.

"Don't be overimpressed, Mr. Henderson," said Lady

Mauley, noting his glances. We'd have given the old ruin to the National Trust years ago if they'd been mad enough to take it. Mind the step there."

"Whut time's ya fren comin'?" asked Tommy, watching Dr. Robbertson put the finishing touches to a plate of sandwiches.

"I told her about half-past four—and her name's Miss Granby, Tommy," said the doctor. "She lived in the States for quite a long time, by the way."

"She purty?" asked Tommy curiously.

"Well, yes, I guess she is. In fact, considering her probable age, she's *very* pretty."

Tommy pried a sandwich apart to investigate the filling.

"An' whut time's Dirk gettin' here, Robbie?" he asked.

Dr. Robbertson almost jerked the plate off the table. "Oh, my God! He *is* coming today, isn't he!" he exclaimed.

"He said Sadday," Tommy replied, chewing contentedly.

"Oh, well," said Dr. Robbertson philosophically, "he knows how to behave."

"Don't *I*?" asked Tommy, his face clouding.

"Oh, of course! Don't be so touchy! I just meant that—there's the bell now."

"Mebbe it's him. Want me ta go?"

"No, I'd better. It may be Miss Granby."

It was.

"What a beastly afternoon!" said Miss Granby after acknowledging her host's greeting. "Oh, thank you. Here, let me put my scarf in the sleeve."

"Come in here, Miss Granby. You're just in time for the last of the old apple tree. It gives a very pretty flame."

"Lovely," Miss Granby agreed, looking at the fire. Then she saw the young man.

"Oh, Miss Granby, this is Tommy Corelli, my nephew from the States. Tommy, this is Miss Granby, my neighbor."

"Howja do, Miss Granby?" said Tommy, producing a bow from God knew where.

"From the States, Mr. Corelli? Where?" asked Miss Granby.

"Syracuse," said Tommy gloomily, shaking back his hair.

"Oh? I've never been there. Is it a pretty city?"

Tommy made a face.

"It's a hole," he said briefly.

"Really?" said Miss Granby, settling herself on the sofa. "That's too bad."

"If I wuz gonna give th' world an enema," Tommy continued, "Syracuse is where I'd stick th' noz—"

"*Aaah*! . . . Tommy doesn't like Syracuse," said the doctor hastily.

"So I gather," replied Miss Granby, hoping that her face was under control. "It sounds rather like my impression of Wilmington—what you'd call a 'hick town': bigots and dreadful moneyed provincials."

Tommy stared innocently at his uncle, who shuddered. Suppose it had been Lela Staine!

During the exchanges of "Strong?" "Sugar, Miss Granby?" the atmosphere became less starchy.

"Have you heard anything further about Lord Mauley?" asked Miss Granby.

"Sir Alistair told me that there're some superficial abrasions and a few rather uncomfortable burns. There's nothing seriously wrong with him, I gather."

"It's chiefly shock, I suppose," said Miss Granby.

"I dare say," the doctor agreed, getting up to stir the fire.

The doorbell rang, and Dr. Robbertson excused himself. Miss Granby smiled encouragingly at Tommy.

"How do you like Cherton, Mr. Corelli?"

"It's reel purty, Miss—Granby? It looks like th' pitchers in my literature book. I ain't—I mean I haven't seen a lot of England. But I think Cherton's reel purty."

What an attractive boy! she thought. That lovely, unspoiled auburn hair! Her ideas were interrupted by the entrance of her host with a young man she had never seen before.

Dr. Robbertson appeared to be having difficulties with his face and his breathing.

"Miss—Miss Granby, this—this is Dirk—er—Mr. Henderson."

Dirk made suitable remarks; then, as the doctor resumed his seat, Dirk crossed to Tommy to exchange a brief handshake and a wink.

Miss Granby looked curiously at the doctor, who was quite red.

"There!" he said at last. "I'm all right! Oh, dear!"

"What has happened?" asked Miss Granby, who felt rather out of things, as did Tommy.

"Dirk brought Lady Mauley to Cherton on his Vespa! Lady Mauley on the rear seat!"

"*Lady* Mauley?" asked Miss Granby, unable to believe that she had heard correctly.

The doctor nodded happily.

"She's a real lady," said Dirk, smiling. "She asked me in for tea—just like I was a friend of hers. And she wanted to give me a fiver!"

"Dinja *take* it?" asked Tommy wonderingly. He didn't know Lady Mauley, but he knew Dirk.

"Of course not! Not after she was so nice to me. I told her I was glad to help her. She's quite a lady!"

"*You* had *tea* at Mauley Hall? With *Lady Mauley*?" asked Dr. Robbertson almost in a whisper.

"Yeh, that's what I just said. That Birkett's a real one, too. At first I thought he was going to show me out the back way when I left, but he didn't. He just smiled at me like I'd given him a—uh—like I'd done something for him, and *he* gave me a fiver." Dirk grinned. "He said he'd belt me one if I didn't take it. He could've, too. What's he weigh? Maybe fifteen stone?"

"Well, Dirk," said the doctor, "you had a profitable trip, it seems."

"Proper Boy Scout, I am. Paid off, too!"

"So Lady Mauley's in Cherton," said Miss Granby musingly. She turned to Tommy. "Lady Mauley feels very much about Cherton, Mr. Corelli, as you seem to feel about Syracuse."

"*Nobody* could feel like me about—"

Dr. Robbertson cut in. "More so," he said, "and Lady Mauley doesn't describe it with Tommy's—ah—delicacy of expression." He laughed. "Tell us everything, Dirk," he went on. "How did you meet Lady Mauley in the first place?"

Miss Granby listened in awe as she heard the story.

"And Miss Pollock?" she asked. "Where's she?"

"The other lady? I suppose she must be at the Hall by now. They sent the car out right away. It's a Rolls, too!"

"Well!" exclaimed Dr. Robbertson.

"Indeed!" said Miss Granby enthusiastically.

"I don't get it," Tommy muttered. "Whut's so funny?"

Dirk moved to the arm of Tommy's chair and tapped him on the shoulder.

"She's an old lady, Tommy. Walks with a stick. Sort of reminds me of pictures of Queen Mary."

"She's nearly ninety-five, Tommy," added Dr. Robbertson.

"Cool! Ninety-five, huh? No wunna you're all excited!"

Presently Miss Granby rose to leave. There had been no occasion to discuss Hopkins, but she did not regret it.

"I don't know when I've enjoyed a visit more, Doctor," she said as she shook hands with him at the door.

"I do hope you'll come again soon," he said seriously. "We'll have to have that chat about Hopkins. Today—well, it seems we had other things to talk about."

"Oh, *today*! Dr. Robbertson, there can never be another day like this one! Not even in Cherton! *Do* thank Mr. Henderson for me! What a boon to conversation!" She dropped her voice. "I think your nephew and Mr. Henderson perfectly charming. So refreshing." Then she laughed. "Lady Mauley!" she exclaimed. "*Please* thank Mr. Henderson for me. I mean it!"

And the smiling Miss Granby disappeared into the thick

and dripping mist. Dr. Robbertson watched her go down the path, and his own smile changed to a grin of satisfaction. Then he sighed. Miss Granby's presence had seemed to cheer Tommy. What of Dirk's? Tommy had first met Dirk shortly after arriving in Cherton.

Dr. Robbertson had not yet fully adjusted to the sudden and unexpected responsibility for an eighteen-year-old nephew, whose mother, the doctor's strong-minded sister, had eloped with a weak-minded but physically gorgeous American bartender. Her husband had survived the boy's birth by less than a year and had left his widow almost destitute. Dr. Robbertson had sent his sister such funds as her pride let her accept, but she had made matters difficult. He had tried to persuade Elizabeth Corelli to return to England, but with a stubbornness he could not yet understand, she had refused his repeated offers. He had been on the verge of visiting Syracuse when word came of her sudden death from pneumonia. The doctor sent long cables of advice, and only three weeks since, the bewildered Tommy had arrived.

Tommy had left school in order to support his mother, but his qualifications were so pitifully few that he had been unable to find a decent job. The doctor was almost sure that the boy had turned in desperation to the only kind of activity that required the sort of capital he had: his striking looks and build. (The doctor did not consider such a profession reprehensible—merely risky.) His nephew's activities had not tainted the fundamental goodness and the shy but genuine sweetness of the boy's nature. The doctor's bitterness toward his sister's strange intransigence was intensified, but he was determined to accept Tommy as he was, with affection and without sanctimoniousness, and to do his best by him. The possibility of getting Tommy into any kind of school was almost hopeless, and for the present he had decided to let matters slide while he learned to know the boy better. He had already discovered that Tommy was proud of his independence. Only by occasional casual references to their blood relationship could the doctor prevail upon the boy to live, for the time being, as his guest. Dr. Robbertson felt that to invoke his legal authority would precipitate disaster—perhaps even a flight to the wilds of London.

It was ironic, he thought as he watched the mist thicken, that after all the villagers' gossip of which he had been the subject, he should find himself in such a situation. Sighing, he closed the door and returned to devise some means of entertaining his young guests.

That Tommy, gentle and sweet though he was, might have thoroughly enjoyed his profession—a promising career, tax-free and physically rewarding—had not yet occurred to Dr. Robbertson.

13

Mr. Staine pushed aside his sermon notes and rose from his desk beside the study fire to stare through the window at the wet and gloomy garden. Then he drew the curtains and began to load his pipe. He did not really enjoy smoking a pipe, but he felt that it reassured and impressed his parishioners. In addition, he had found that the business of stuffing it, tamping it, lighting it (repeatedly), and knocking it out (often) provided those extra moments he required to arrange his occasional thoughts. It was particularly useful at vestry meetings, and Mr. Staine was fully aware of how effective was his gesture of rubbing the briar along the side of his nose as he considered a statement he did not really understand.

"Tea, Frederick!" came his wife's voice.

He picked up his matches and tobacco pouch and strolled into the drawing room.

"Ha! What a cheerful conflagration! Most comforting, the creature comforts, my dear Lela."

He sat down and took the cup from his wife.

"Could you find the wool you wanted to match?" he asked.

"Of course not. That wretched Barnes never has anything one wants. They've got to send to London for it."

"Too bad," said the vicar. "It was a depressing afternoon to drive to Porford for nothing."

"Well, it wasn't *completely* fruitless. I *did* get that large tin of pineapple that Simms wanted." Mrs. Staine sipped her Darjeeling and frowned. She looked at her husband. "How is Lord Mauley?"

"Why, I told him this morning that I'd stop by after dinner. I haven't seen him since I saw you."

"You aren't having tea at the Hall, then?"

"No, Lela, dear. I'm having tea here," he said, putting down his cup.

Mrs. Staine glared at her husband.

"I *mean,* Frederick, that you don't intend to go to the Hall for a late-afternoon visit. I am *quite* aware that you're having tea *here*!"

"Well, I'm going to the Hall after dinner, Lela."

"So you said before," remarked Mrs. Staine in an irritated tone.

Simms came into the drawing room.

"Lady Mauley is on the line, Mrs. Staine. Her ladyship would like to speak to the vicar."

It was well that Mr. Staine was not holding his cup. He dropped only his pipe, and, as it was going nicely, glowing ashes spilled over the silk rug beneath the table.

"Oh, Frederick! That abominable pipe! No, no! Let it alone! I'll do it. You go to the telephone. Don't keep Lady Mauley waiting!"

The vicar almost scuttled from the room. *Why* hadn't someone told him that Lady Mauley was in Cherton? Not a word had been said about it that morning! He picked up the telephone as if it were a grenade. He cleared his throat to adjust his register.

"Ah, Lady Mauley! This is *indeed* a pleasant surprise!"

At the other end of the line Lady Mauley held the instrument at arm's length and stared at it with distaste. Then she sighed and returned it to her ear.

"Thank you, Vicar. I've only just arrived. My idiot son tells me you've been quite—attentive—in your attendance."

"Ah—um—that's very kind of your—of Lord Mauley. I was only too glad to be of help."

"Umgh! Well, I understand you're expected to call tonight," said Lady Mauley. To the vicar her voice sounded like a purr. Perhaps that was because he could not see her face.

"Why, yes, Lady Mauley. I—just thought I'd—just drop by—just to see if I'm needed, you know."

"Yes. I know. Well, I *just* thought I'd save you the trouble, Vicar. I *just* hate your putting yourself out for nothing. Sister Benson seems to be quite able, and I really feel that you'd *just* do better to remain at home. Such a dreadful night, you know."

"Oh, it's *no* trouble at *all,* Lady Mauley," said the vicar in his best deathbedside manner.

"*Much* too much trouble. So, thank you, Vicar. Have a quiet, warm evening at home. We shan't expect you. *Good* night, Vicar!"

Mr. Staine stood for some minutes with the telephone pressed against his ear. Finally, he shook his head, found that the instrument impeded the motion, and replaced it on its cradle. He wandered slowly back to the drawing room.

"*How* is *dear* Lady Mauley?" asked Mrs. Staine solicitously.

Mr. Staine shook his head gloomily.

"Just as usual," he said. "An extraordinary woman, really!"

"I suppose she's going to send the car for you?"

Mr. Staine winced.

"Um—Lady Mauley very kindly insisted that I not—ah—discommode myself this evening—because of the weather, you know."

"Oh, how *thoughtful* of her!" exclaimed Mrs. Staine.

"Ah—yes. Yes, wasn't it?"

"Julia?"

"This is she."

"This is Emily Mauley. I'm here for a few days. You must have dinner with me tomorrow."

"Thank you, Lady Mauley. I heard you'd arrived. Unfortunately, I have to go up to London for a concert tomorrow. I don't expect to be back until sometime after six."

"Oh, nonsense, Julia! You can do without a concert. I shall expect you."

"That's good of you, Lady Mauley, but the concert can't do without *me*. I'm playing in it."

"Oh! . . . Well, in that case we'll plan for a bit later. You'll be back about six o'clock, you say?"

"Yes, but—"

"Good! We'll pick you up about seven or a little before."

"But I can walk, Lady Mauley."

"Perhaps you can, but I can't—at least not to Wroxley. Agnes and I shall see you about seven. We shall have dinner at that excellent little French place in Wroxley. You don't think I'd ask you eat the provender *here*, do you?"

"Well," said Mrs. Dodridge, defeated, "that will be most pleasant. I shall be ready."

"Splendid. Do you think Thelma Mullen would like to join us?"

Would Thelma? There might be time to warn her if she could reach her when Lady Mauley rang off.

"Why—probably. I don't know whether she's engaged or not."

"I'll ask her. Good night, Julia."

"Good night, Lady Mauley. And—thank you."

Mrs. Dodridge dialed and was pleased when her friend answered. Briefly, she explained the situation to Lady Thelma.

"What fun! You're really going, Julia?"

"Did you ever try to persuade Lady Mauley against her convictions, Thelma? She decided that I was going, and so—I'm going."

"I'll accept to keep you in spirits. Really, Julia, you know you adore the woman!"

"Of course I do. It's just that I don't like to be made to

feel that I've no mind of my own, while she has enough for two."

"Well, she certainly didn't pass any of it on to Charlie!"

"Very well, Thelma. I'll see you in high state tomorrow."

14

The Right Reverend Charles Dodridge pressed violently upon the brake pedal and only barely avoided a collision with a wildly careering motorcycle.

"His is the assurance of perfect faith or the indifference of total despair," he muttered. He relaxed and completed the turn into his sister-in-law's drive.

He smiled as Edwards opened the door.

"Good afternoon, Edwards. Is Mrs. Dodridge here?"

"Oh! Good afternoon, my lord. I—I'm afraid that Mrs. Dodridge has gone up to London. There's a concert there this afternoon."

"I *knew* I should have telephoned!" exclaimed the bishop. "When will she be back?"

"About six, I think, my lord. Won't you come in, sir?"

"Yes. Just let me get my bag."

"Oh, I'll get it, my lord!"

"Nonsense, Edwards! It weighs as much as you do. You can let me have some tea, I dare say?"

"Yes, my lord. And I've just made some cakes."

Edwards watched disapprovingly as the bishop carried his bag from the car to the house.

"I'll light the fire in the drawing room. Is there anything you'd like, sir?"

"No, Edwards—except your cakes and tea. They sound like a splendid idea. Such a misty, cold afternoon! I'll do a bit of washing up and then go in and enjoy the fire."

Edwards lighted the fire and retired to her kitchen. She looked at the clock. It was only half-past four. She shrugged, put on the kettle, and looked into the oven. As she shut it, she heard the telephone.

"Oh, Edwards. This is Lady Thelma. Would you ask Mrs. Dodridge to call me as soon as she returns, please? I'm not sure what time Lady Mauley is to come for us."

"Yes, ma'am," said Edwards. "Oh—ma'am?"

"What is it, Edwards?"

"The bishop's just come, ma'am. We didn't expect him. I—I thought, knowing his lordship and your ladyship are such good friends, I—I thought maybe you'd like to know."

"Why, thank you for telling me, Edwards. Is the bishop just sitting there by himself?"

"Yes, ma'am. I'm making tea for him. He—his lordship said he wasn't—I mean, he said he wished he'd rung."

"Tell the bishop that I called and that I shall stroll over and have tea with him." To Lady Thelma, Edwards sounded almost desperate, as indeed she was.

"Oh, yes, ma'am! That'll be lovely, ma'am. I'll tell his lordship at once."

"Well, Charles, this is a surprise!"

"I'm the one who's surprised, Thelma. I completely forgot about this blessed concert. I remember now that Julia mentioned its being on the fourteenth. Stupid of me not to've telephoned."

"How is Margaret?" asked Lady Thelma.

"Quite well. She's visiting her mother in Kent at the moment and has taken both children with her. That's why I'm able to pay Julia this little visit. The Palace is very dull for even a temporary bachelor."

Lady Thelma looked expressively at the bishop.

"I hope Julia won't let you feel lonely," she said. "You *must* join our little party tonight."

"Thelma, I don't like that grin of yours. What little party?"

"Lady Mauley is here, and she's asked Julia and me to

have dinner in Wroxley with her and Agnes Pollock. I'm sure she'd be delighted to have you join us.''

The bishop raised his eyebrows.

''I wonder if I'm up to coping with Lady Mauley today. She's delightful, of course, but I had an interminable confirmation service this morning. I do so wish that the young men wouldn't put all that oil or lard or whatever it is on their hair.''

Lady Thelma laughed.

''There's no prohibition in the Prayer Book, is there?''

''Unfortunately not. And I don't know how many wigs I introduced into the mystical body of Christ's church. Indeed, I suspect some of the young men of wearing them, too.''

''Oh, well. Youth! At least they're taking an interest in their appearance. *You* wouldn't disapprove of that, Charles.''

''Indeed I wouldn't. I'm not so stuffy as that, I hope. In fact, I have several clergymen in the diocese who'd be none the worse for a few false lovelocks. No, it's just that I shan't be able to wear those vestments again until they've been properly cleaned. Oh, well. What is the news in Cherton, Thelma?''

''News? In Cherton? Really, Charles, you should know better! And yet . . .'' Lady Thelma paused for effect, ''. . . we *do* have news of a sort. Charlie Mauley is hors de combat owing to an unequal dispute with a towel heater, and his mother arrived last night on the rear seat of a motorbicycle in the company of a young man whom most of the villagers would cut dead were they willing to acknowledge his existence at all.''

''Thelma, you're deliberately building up a story,'' said the bishop reprovingly. ''Stop the nonsense and tell me the truth.''

''But I *am* telling you the truth! Charlie is flat on his back with burns, and his mother appeared in Cherton in company with one of Dr. Robbertson's protégés.''

''No!'' exclaimed the bishop, enthralled.

''Yes!'' replied Lady Thelma. ''And here's tea. Why, Edwards! You've outdone yourself! What lovely-looking little cakes! Shall I pour, Charles?''

Reddening with pleasure, Edwards deposited the tray and left.

As she managed the teacups, Lady Thelma told the story of Lord Mauley's unfortunate accident and the subsequent arrival of his mother.

"Charles, if you laugh like that and try to eat, you're going to kill yourself."

The bishop could only shake his head. Finally, he managed to subside to a chuckle and said, "'It is the Lord's doing and is marvelous in our eyes'."

"I doubt that the Lord had much to do with it," said Lady Thelma. Then she paused. "But perhaps he did. I can quote, too, you know: 'He hath put down the mighty from their seats and exalted those of low degree.'"

"Hmm," said the bishop.

"Especially the last part. Do you know that this beleathered lad had tea with Lady Mauley—at the Hall?"

"Beautiful!" exclaimed the bishop. "Have you met him?"

"No, but I should dearly like to."

"Wait," said the bishop, recollecting. "Is this chap a young slender fellow with very long auburn hair?"

"I've not even seen him, Charles. Why?"

"Because I've just remembered. I nearly ran down a Vespa as I drove in here. Perhaps it was he."

"Perhaps. It could have been."

"'His driving is like the driving of Jehu, son of Nimshi, for he driveth furiously,'" said the bishop, shaking his head. "How is Robbie, by the way?" he added.

"As insouciant as ever."

"Still painting?"

"Yes," replied Lady Thelma, grinning.

"You know, Thelma, he does very good work. He's by no means so bad as Julia pretends. I've seen some of his landscapes, and there is a real feeling for nature in them. Not Constable, of course, but quite good—sound workmanship." The bishop thought for a moment, then continued. "As for those life studies, whether you like that sort of thing or not, they're extraordinarily well done, although I grant you that some of them are pretty strong meat. How are the Staines? Still the same, I suppose."

"Naturally. Or, rather, unnaturally. You didn't expect some sort of miracle, did you, Charles? And the Hitchcocks—and Fanny Granby. All in our little circle are just as cozy—and circuitous—as ever." Lady Thelma sighed. "Julia and I were puzzling just the other morning over why we live in Cherton. Neither of us came up with a really satisfactory answer."

"I suppose not. It's rather like asking a man why he has to drink. If he really knew, he could probably stop. Do you think you could leave Cherton if you knew why you apparently can't?"

Lady Thelma frowned in thought as she poured herself another cup of tea.

"I think, Thelma, you're giving the matter more consideration than it's worth," said the bishop with a smile.

"No," said Lady Thelma. "It's just that I'm not sure I think your analogy a good one, Charles, although living here and dipsomania *may* be synonymous. After all, it's a wonder that Cherton isn't peopled exclusively with alcoholics."

"Perhaps, Thelma. But alcoholism seems to be a disease, and I think that living in Cherton is a disease, too."

"You're still wrong, Charles, if you'll forgive me. Living in Cherton isn't a disease. It's a symptom. But what is it a symptom *of*?"

The bishop considered.

"An inordinate if unconscious craving for martyrdom," he concluded.

Lady Thelma looked at her watch.

"Julia should be home soon," she said. "I was quite serious about tonight. I'm sure Lady Mauley would be glad to see you. Won't you join us?"

"My dear Thelma! I'm a tired man seeking a moment's respite. Dinner with Lady Mauley is not my idea of a respite, charming though she undoubtedly is. No, I shall ask Julia to give me some sort of dinner, and while you and she are reveling in Lady Mauley, I shall go over some of the diocesan papers I have with me."

"And that's your idea of a respite?" asked Lady Thelma acidly. "Very well. I shan't say another word. I shall merely content myself with observing that I detect serious evidence of moral cowardice in the incumbent of the See of Wroxminster.''

''How right you are. Where Lady Mauley is concerned, I'm an utter craven.''

''I think I hear the car,'' said Lady Thelma.

In a moment Mrs. Dodridge appeared, still in her coat and hat and holding a portfolio.

''Charles! What a charming surprise! Edwards said that you and Thelma were here. You were really remiss in not telephoning, but I'm glad you didn't, for then you might not have come. I hope you've nothing planned for tonight?''

Lady Thelma and the bishop exchanged grins.

''Oh,'' said Mrs. Dodridge. ''I see you've been warned. Very well. I *was* going to telephone Lady Mauley, but you can stay here with some of James's port and catch up on your reading. I do hope you don't have to hurry off tomorrow?''

''I can stay until Thursday, Julia, though I shall have to spend Tuesday at Porford. But, really, *do* you want me to go with you tonight? I shall if you both insist.''

''We don't insist at all,'' said Mrs. Dodridge, removing her coat, hat, and gloves. ''After all, even a bishop is not immune to the attractions that a weak-willed self-indulgence offers. I shall tell Edwards to bring up the port. You *do* like boiled tripe, don't you? With brandied turnips?''

''Oh, all right!'' groaned the bishop. ''You might just as well be Margaret!''

15

''Bishop, you sit here by me. Julia? Pull out the seat. It's abominably uncomfortable, but I've had worse rides. Agnes? You sit on the seat next to Julia, and Thelma and the bishop can sit back here with me. Cartwright? Where's Cartwright?''

''Here, ma'am,'' said Terry Cartwright, presenting himself.

"You know the way to Wroxley, young man?" asked Lady Mauley, whom Smith had rendered eternally sceptical.

"Yes, m'lady."

"You're *sure*?"

"Yes, m'lady. I was born there."

"Umgh! Very well. We want to go to the Blue Flag."

Cartwright was hopelessly frank.

"I—I don't know it, m'lady, but I'll find it," he said. He was in but his second month of Lord Mauley's erratic employ.

"If you were *born* there, you *must* know," said Lady Mauley, her distrust reawakening. "It's a little place on Cobb Street—has very good food."

"Oh!" exclaimed Cartwright. "Le Drapeau Bleu!"

The bishop laughed. Cartwright's accent was impeccable.

After a moment, Lady Mauley also laughed, placing her hand upon the young man's shoulder.

"Cartwright, don't you know, then, that 'le drapeau bleu' means 'the blue flag'?"

Cartwright crimsoned.

"I—I guess I did, m'lady, but I was thinking of Red Lions and White Harts."

"Do you speak French?" asked Lady Thelma curiously.

"Yes, ma'am. My mother's from Toulon. She and my father own Le Drapeau Bleu."

"Que faites-vous dans le service de mon fils?" Lady Mauley demanded with asperity.

Cartwright grinned.

"Je déteste faire la cuisine, madame la vicomtesse. Mon père m'a fichu à la porte il y a deux ans."

"Zut!" said Lady Mauley. Then she smiled. "See me tomorrow, Cartwright. I think that I should talk to you."

"Yes, m'lady."

Eventually everyone settled down in the car, and Cartwright closed the doors. Miss Pollock, in spite of her long experience with her cousin, was still in a state of semishock as a result of the Vespa incident. She was relieved to see that Cartwright, who could not have been more than nineteen, handled the car with an assurance totally foreign to the hopeless Smith. (That worthy was in bed, buttressed by hot-water bottles, cheered by a fire of the best household coal, and invigorated by an endless supply of hot whiskey punch.) Miss Pollock did not know the bishop, but she knew Mrs. Dodridge and Lady Thelma, and she leaned back in her seat, determined to enjoy the evening.

Upon entering the rather cramped dining parlor of Le Drapeau Bleu, Lady Thelma and Mrs. Dodridge had eyes for only one table. At it were seated Dr. Robbertson and two young men, one of whom grinned as Lady Mauley came in.

"Why, it's Mr. Henderson!" exclaimed Lady Mauley.

"Oh, my God!" said Miss Pollock under her breath.

Lady Mauley's guests looked at her quizzically.

"It's that delightful young man who brought me to Cherton! We must make a party of it! Waiter? Mr.—Cartwright? Put this table together with that gentleman's. We'll all have dinner together. *So* pleasant to see you again, Doctor! Mr. Henderson! What a fortunate meeting was ours! I shall always be grateful for your kindness."

Dr. Robbertson had already observed Mrs. Dodridge's startled look and Lady Thelma's half-suppressed grin. He got up graciously, nudging Tommy to rise.

"And who is this young man?" asked Lady Mauley, smiling at Tommy.

The doctor made the necessary introductions and shook hands with the bishop, who then shook hands with the two youths. Lady Thelma and Mrs. Dodridge smiled in acknowledgment. Miss Pollock smiled in disbelief. She was simply numb.

"Well!" said Lady Mauley, settling herself. "Now *what* shall we have? Have you ordered, Doctor?"

"No, we were just about to have a drink, Lady Mauley."

"Splendid! *Well,* then! You shall all be my guests. Not a *word! No* discussion! They have a superb pâté de maison here. I think we shall have a large—you hear that, waiter?—

a *large* terrine of pâté." Lady Mauley looked happily about her. "Now what would you like to drink?"

Dazedly or composedly, they gave their orders, Dr. Robbertson ordering a gin and tonic for his nephew.

"Thelma," whispered Mrs. Dodridge behind the cover of an eighteen-inch menu, "I can't believe it's happening."

"Don't even try," Lady Thelma whispered back. "You'll have to believe more later on, if I know our hostess. Save your strength."

"Oysters!" exclaimed Lady Mauley. "Oysters would be nice, I think. Does everyone like oysters?"

Everyone liked oysters—except Tommy.

"Now, let me see. Do you still have those lovely fried scampi? Yes? Splendid! Does everyone like scampi?"

Everyone apparently adored scampi—except Tommy.

"Hmm—chicken—beef—veal—lamb—pork. What would you like? Would everyone like roast beef?"

The bishop could bear it no longer.

"I should like the capon in white wine," he said grimly.

Lady Thelma smiled.

"May I have the veau Niçoise?" she asked. "They do it so well here."

"Any other dissidents?" asked Lady Mauley, eyeing them. "I was beginning to think that you have neither tastes nor minds of your own."

"Well," said Dr. Robbertson, who was getting his bearings, "I should like the roast beef, but I think I'd prefer the American clams to oysters. The cherrystones."

Lady Mauley nodded approval and smiled at Dirk.

"I'd like the chicken in wine, ma'am," he said, grinning.

"Agnes?"

"Zigeunerschnitzel!" snarled Miss Pollack.

"Julia?"

"I think I should like the truite aux amandes, Lady Mauley."

Tommy whispered to his uncle, "D'ya think I could have a cheeseburger an' onion, Robbie?"

"You try it, and I'll disembowel you with a dull knife when we get home!" Dr. Robbertson whispered back between his teeth.

Tommy didn't know what "disembowel" meant, but the "dull knife" sounded threatening, so he compromised on roast beef when Lady Mauley turned to him and, in a surprisingly gentle tone, asked him what he wanted.

Exhausted and nearly distraught, the waiter decamped to the kitchen.

" 'Oo's that old witch?" he asked Mrs. Cartwright.

Cartwright had been talking to his mother, and the waiter was answered by both with a torrent of Gallic invective that made him glad to return to the comparative geniality of the dining parlor. He arrived, laden with drinks, in time to hear the conclusion of an oration by the Lady Patroness.

". . . never," Lady Mauley was saying, "never shall I forget the experience of yesterday. Mr. Henderson, you realize, I trust, the magnificent opportunities of your generation? Opportunities that were denied my own."

Dirk looked baffled, and the bishop intervened.

"Yet, Lady Mauley," he said, "perhaps *your* generation has experienced even more."

"How is that, Bishop?"

"Why—do you remember the first time you used a telephone, Lady Mauley? The first time you heard the wireless? Or saw television? And—if you've flown—the first time you boarded an aeroplane? Think of all these things that Mr. Henderson and Mr. Corelli take for granted. How long should we have been coming to Wroxley from Cherton eighty years ago?"

"Yes, Bishop," said Lady Mauley, nodding in agreement. "You're partly right, of course. But, you see, I was a grown woman, even an *old* woman, when many of these things came into being. It's the freshness of youth, the ability to accept them *as* commonplace, that I envy. Why, *I'm* still awed by a gramophone record! How do you expect me to feel when I think of this young man's compatriots"—she bowed graciously to Tommy—"actually *walking* on the moon? My dear Bishop, in my day the moon was something to which one's suitors wrote poetry."

Tommy smiled uncertainly at Lady Mauley. She returned his smile, and he grew more cheerful. He felt badly out of his element, and he was anxious not to disgrace his uncle. Dr. Robbertson sensed this and slipped a protective arm behind the boy, who snuggled trustingly against it.

The waiter came and went, changing plates and glasses. At last Lady Mauley sighed.

"*Very* good!" she remarked.

There was a chorus of agreement.

"Now *what* shall we have for pudding?" she asked brightly.

The silence was leaden.

"A liqueur with our coffee, then?" she asked.

"Grand Marnier," said the bishop, "would be rather pleasant, I think."

"Speak up, now! *Do!*" said Lady Mauley graciously.

They named their choices, Dr. Robbertson ordering a Drambuie for Tommy before the boy could ask for beer.

As they rose to leave, Lady Mauley issued an invitation that electrified Miss Pollock.

"I shall expect you all for tea at the Hall tomorrow afternoon. You've already told me, Dr. Robbertson, that Mr. Henderson will be here for several days, and I know, Bishop, that *you're* not leaving until Thursday. I shall expect you *all. Just* this little group. *And,* Mr. Henderson, I want you to bring your motorbicycle. I think that the bishop would enjoy trying it. My son has quite a good road through the park."

As the bishop and Mrs. Dodridge passed through the latter's front door, the bishop chuckled.

"Well, Julia, you were right. Both you and Thelma. I *did* have a most pleasant time. Ah—let's have some whiskey, shall we?"

"Have what you like, Charles. *I'm* going to have a Zombie!"

16

"Birkett?"

"Yes, sir?"

"What's the time?"

"Half-past ten, sir."

"Is—is my mother here?"

"No, sir. Lady Mauley and Miss Pollock have gone to the funeral at St. Margaret's, sir."

"Funeral, Birkett?"

"Yes, sir. The little West baby is being buried today."

"Oh. It's—it's dead?"

"Yes—sir," said Birkett with an effort. "Dead, sir."

"Umm." Lord Mauley meditated. Then he said, "It's such a pity, Birkett, you know."

"Yes, sir, it is. The third child poor Mrs. West has buried in as many years."

"Umm—yes. Well—I meant—well, it's such a pity that babies always seem to die so young."

"*Sir?* . . . Oh, yes. Yes, sir. Quite so, sir." Birkett paused, breathing heavily. "Will there be anything else, sir?"

"No. Oh, where is the *Times*?"

"On your chest, sir."

"Oh, yes. Well, that will be all, Birkett."

"Yes, sir."

Birkett shut the door quietly behind him. Then he sighed and went downstairs to find the housekeeper.

"Mrs. Payne, I'm going for a walk. If Lord Mauley wishes anything in my absence, tell Whittaker to see to it. I shall be back shortly."

"Very well, Mr. Birkett. How is his lordship this morning?"

"The same," said Birkett mournfully.
"Oh, that's too bad!" said Mrs. Payne.
"Yes, it is."

At the south end of Mauley Park, on a slight eminence, stood a folly built in the last quarter of the eighteenth century by the third Viscount Mauley, who had seen fit to combine in the structure the worst characteristics of Flamboyant with the most depraved excesses of the Corinthian order. A spire only three feet lower than that of Salisbury Cathedral rose from a two-storied marble portico of liver-colored pillars. For years, the thing had been known to the irreverent as His Lordship's Only Erection.

To this folly it was Birkett's habit to retire when he felt unduly put upon. This particular morning it was not so much Lord Mauley, for his employer was very much the same as usual. Nor was it the thought of the West child, for the little creature's death had been a certainty for some days. It was Cartwright. He was a good lad, but his youthful sense of humor occasionally betrayed him into a certain callousness, and when he had gleefully informed Birkett (before breakfast, too) of the impending arrival of Dr. Robbertson, Henderson, et alii, Birkett had been compelled to take the young fellow down a peg or two. When Lady Mauley later confirmed Cartwright's information, the shock was rendered more severe by the knowledge that he had unjustly reprimanded the lad. Birkett sighed again as he sauntered along the walk, savoring in spite of himself the promise of spring in the damp bright air, and wondering how he could apologize to Cartwright without compromising his butlerian dignity.

Upon reaching the folly, Birkett mounted the stairs leading to a narrow observation gallery and turned to survey the countryside. It was a lovely day. Lady Mauley and Miss Pollock had returned from the church, he noticed. They were walking about the East Parterre, the old lady waving her stick as she talked. To the west, he could see the vicar cycling along the road to the Hall gate, head bowed in abstraction. All seemed peaceful and normal. Birkett felt depressed.

He had taken out a cigar and had struck a match when he heard the sound of a motorbicycle. In a moment he could see a well-known Vespa coming on toward the vicar, from the opposite direction. The vicar seemed lost to all worldly cares, and as the Vespa approached around a curve, he allowed his bicycle to wobble directly into the path of the oncoming vehicle. The driver of the Vespa—obviously Henderson—swerved wildly to miss the vicar. In this he succeeded, although he was hampered in his movements by his fellow rider, another young man, who, hair flying, was clinging devotedly to Henderson's waist. It was too much for the vicar, however. He fell to the ground, landing on his back, and the bicycle burrowed into the hedge by the road. The Vespa came to a halt slightly beyond the recumbent incumbent, and the two young men hastily dismounted.

Birkett grinned as Henderson helped the vicar to his feet.

"The young devil!" he exclaimed. Then he swore as the match burned his fingers. He dropped it, stuffed the cigar back into his pocket, and ran down the stairs toward the Hall.

"*Frederick!* What on *earth*—"

"*Abominable! Utterly* abominable!"

"*What* has *happened,* Frederick? You're simply *covered* with mud!"

The vicar closed his eyes and endeavored to control himself. Then he pushed past his wife and hobbled up the stairs.

"A—a young fool on one of those damnable motorbicycles! Tried to kill me! *Wait* until I see that—that Robbertson *person*!"

Mrs. Staine was at a loss.

"Dr. Robbertson?"

The vicar snarled.

"Then some ass in a black saloon stopped to say he'd seen it! Said it was *my* fault! Nearly killed by one of those—goddamned *bloody concubines*!"

"FREDERICK!"

"Abominable!" said the vicar, disappearing into the bathroom.

His wife followed him to the door.

"Who was the man who stopped?" she asked.

"I neither know nor care!" snapped her husband. "I scarcely looked at him. How *could* I with my eyes full of mud?"

"But—Dr. Robbertson?"

"I prefer not to discuss the matter further, Lela. There are *some* things! All this bloody permissiveness! *Please* allow me to disrobe and cleanse myself?"

"Oh, yes! Of course! Only—"

"God*damn* you, woman!" the vicar shouted. "Will you get the bloody fuck *out* of here!"

"You could not have possibly done anything except what you did, Mr. Henderson," said the bishop gravely. "The man rode directly across your path."

"I suppose not, my lord," said Dirk ruefully. "I'm glad you happened along, sir. That chap could make things hot for me."

"Do you know who it was, then?" asked the bishop. "He seemed familiar, but he was so covered with mud that I couldn't be sure."

Before Dirk could reply, Tommy spoke, looking anxiously at his friend. "It wuz th' preacher here. Name's Staine."

The bishop pressed his hand to his head.

"Oh, dear heaven!" he murmured. "Yes, of course. It *would* be!"

"Wuzzat, sir?" asked Tommy curiously.

"Oh—oh, nothing." The bishop shook his head and compressed his lips. Then he said, "Mr. Henderson, if you have any trouble at all about this, kindly let me know. I shall be more than willing to corroborate your evidence."

"Thank you, my lord," said Dirk gratefully.

"And you, young man," said the bishop in a kindly tone as

he turned to Tommy, "you be more careful. I believe it was you I nearly ran down yesterday afternoon—turning into Mrs. Dodridge's drive."

Tommy flushed.

"I'll be careful, sir," he said contritely. "I'm sorry I got in ya way."

"Well, you're a good-looking young man," said the bishop, smiling, "and you'll be much more attractive if you remain in one piece. Still, no serious harm was done, and, as I said, Mr. Henderson, if you have difficulty, please get in touch with me."

Dirk thanked him again, and the bishop got into his car and went his way.

Tommy looked at Dirk.

"D'ya think th' bishop was mad, Dirk?"

"Well, no. He seemed to think something was pretty funny. Didn't you think so?"

"Yeh. Guess I'll never figger you English out."

"Are you going to stay in England, Tommy?"

"Guess I hafta. Robbie's th' only relative I got, only . . ." Tommy paused, his face troubled.

"What's the matter, sweetie?" asked Dirk.

"Well, Robbie's a good guy. He's been awful nice ta me. Bought me a lotta clo'es an' new shoes an' things, but—"

"What's wrong with that?"

"Hell, Dirk, I can't keep on takin' stuff from him! I got *plenty* of money, but he won't let me spend it! I can't keep on spongin' on him. I gotta get where I can *work*!"

Dirk eyed him with amusement.

"I suppose Cherton *doesn't* have much of a market! You'd have to go up to London."

"Yeh. Mebbe we can talk about an idea I got, but I wanta wait a while first."

"You haven't seen London yet, have you, Tommy? We'll have to go up there some weekend. A chap I know is always looking for male fashion models. You'd make a perfect clotheshorse."

"Ya think so, Dirk?" asked Tommy doubtfully. *Wearing* clothes to make money? He thought it sounded dull.

Mrs. Dodridge rose from her seat at the harpsichord as her brother-in-law entered the drawing room.

"Oh, there you are! Would you like to have some coffee?"

"Julia, I should like to have a glass of Madeira."

"Of course, Charles. Is—is anything wrong?"

"No, no, my dear, not really. Just—just one of the diocesan problems. But I should like a glass of Madeira."

17

Cartwright cautiously entered the sitting room. Lady Mauley, he had been told, was "unpredictable."

She watched him approach her chair and smiled. He was very young.

"Now, Cartwright," she said, "what's all this nonsense about not wanting to cook?"

"I—I just don't think I'd like it, m'lady," he said nervously, unconsciously rumpling his fine blond hair as he twisted his black brows in a puzzled frown.

"But how can you tell until you've *tried* it? How do you know that you can't do it?"

"Oh, I can *do* it, m'lady. I *have* tried it. It's just that—well, you see, m'lady, you spend all that time preparing a dinner, and then all your work's gobbled up—in an hour or less. It seems so pointless, ma'am."

"Pointless! Food *pointless*? And your mother is a Frenchwoman!"

"That—that's what my father says, m'lady."

"Sit down, Cartwright," said Lady Mauley in a tone that brooked no refusal. "You're making me fidgety. Do you smoke?"

"Yes, m'lady."

"Then light a cigarette," said Lady Mauley.

Cartwright complied, and Lady Mauley settled herself more comfortably.

"Young man," she said, "smoking is an injurious and disgusting habit!"

"Yes, m'lady."

"You're *much* too handsome to spoil your teeth and lungs with nicotine. Er—are those Gauloises?"

"Yes, m'lady."

"Please give me one. I'm told they're vile, but that they *do* have character."

Cartwright lighted Lady Mauley's cigarette, and she inhaled appreciatively. The next second, she was half out of her chair, exploding in a fit of coughing. She waved off the concern of the young man.

"Water!" she croaked. "In the carafe—on the writing table there!"

For several moments, she continued to hoot and hack while Cartwright looked worriedly at her and at the door.

"My word!" she exclaimed at last. "No wonder you don't like to cook! How can you possibly taste *anything* if you smoke these revolting objects?"

"That's what my mother says, m'lady."

"It appears to me," said Lady Mauley, now tolerably sure that she could speak without risking an internal rupture, "that you have two very sensible parents. Do you realize, Cartwright, that there's a gold mine at your very feet? You probably know that Le Drapeau Bleu is famous all over this part of England?"

"Yes, m'lady."

"Cartwright, you're a dunce!"

He flushed, shuffling his feet uneasily.

Lady Mauley relented.

"But a charming dunce," she said. "Cartwright, I'm going to make a suggestion. Would you like to be my chauffeur for a year or two? And promise me to think over in the meanwhile the wisdom of refusing to join your parents?"

Cartwright's mouth dropped open.

"Don't goggle at me like an unfledged sparrow waiting for a worm, young man! Think over what I've said. I shall be returning to Maulcaster in a few days. If you want to come with me as my chauffeur, I should like to engage you. My present chauffeur is retiring—*has* retired, though the old fool doesn't know it yet. I must break it to him gently, I think."

Cartwright could not imagine Lady Mauley gently breaking anything to anybody.

She seemed to read his mind.

"I'm not really such a bear, you know," she said with a smile. "Oh, I growl at people, but those who know me know just what it's worth." She looked pensively across the room; then she looked back at the youth. "I don't like fools, Cartwright. That's rather an unfortunate attitude for anyone who has to come near Cherton, isn't it?" He was not sure he was supposed to reply to this, but Lady Mauley went on. "However, this little visit has been *quite* productive. I've met one or two very interesting people."

"Yes, m'lady," said Cartwright noncommittally.

"Well? Do you think you'd like to go to Maulcaster?"

"Oh, *yes,* m'lady!"

"Very well. You'll find the wages good and the duties almost nominal. I rarely go out, but when I need you, I shall want you instantly at hand. Is that understood?"

"Yes, m'lady."

"And you promise to try to reconsider your idiotic decision about Le Drapeau Bleu?"

"I'll—I'll try, ma'am, but—"

"All I ask is that you honestly *try,* Cartwright."

"Yes, m'lady."

"Good! I think that will be all for now, young man. I shall let you know in a day or so when I plan to leave. I don't think the car will be ready before Thursday. Will that give you time enough?"

"Oh, yes, m'lady," said Cartwright, rising.

"I shall arrange matters with my son. Now will you please ask someone to tell Miss Pollock that I should like to see her?"

Cartwright left the sitting room, determined to find the fool who had called Lady Mauley "unpredictable." It was not until he was downstairs that he discovered he had left his cigarettes on Lady Mauley's sewing table.

Miss Pollock entered a room filled with clouds of stinking smoke. In the haze was what sounded like the hectic hacking of an elderly mammal in the final stages of consumption.

"Cousin Emily!"

"Water! In the carafe—on the writing table there!"

18

Dr. Robbertson was about to dial Miss Granby's number when the telephone rang. He gave a slight start and picked up the instrument.

"Robbertson here."

"Ah, Doctor," intoned a plangent voice that he knew only too well. He grinned.

"Oh, hello, Vicar. I do hope you're not too badly shaken up after your accident this morning."

"Ah, yes. . . . Yes. I—um—I wish to speak to you about that, Doctor," said Mr. Staine, clearing his throat preparatory to a descent in pitch.

Dr. Robbertson took advantage of the vicar's vocalization to strike the first blow.

"Henderson tells me you had quite a nasty fall," he said. "Even though he apparently couldn't have avoided upsetting you, I'm glad he didn't actually hit you. Evidently, he wasn't really at fault."

There was a shocked gurgle.

"Not at *fault*, Doctor? Do you realize that that irresponsible young—man—nearly killed me?"

"Oh, now come off it, Vicar! Bishop Dodridge assured me that you were totally on the wrong side of the road."

"*I* was on the—uh? *Ainh? What* did you say? Bishop Dodridge?"

"Why, yes. Didn't you speak to the bishop when he stopped his car to help you?"

The response at the other end of the line was nil. Dr. Robbertson struggled to keep his laughter silent and winked at Dirk and Tommy lounging in pagan abandon on the posing platform. He knew perfectly well that the nonrecognition had been mutual, but he had no intention of letting the vicar off easily.

"Vicar? Are you there?"

"Glgnk!"

"I beg your pardon?" said Dr. Robbertson.

"Bishop—Dodridge? Was—was that who that was?" The vicar's voice had exchanged plangency for a hoarse and most unecclesiastical squawk.

Dr. Robbertson permitted himself a slight laugh.

"Do you *mean*, Vicar, that you didn't recognize *your own bishop?*"

"Ah—um. Yes," said the vicar, trying desperately to remember *what* he had said to his superior. Of course, he had been under a frightful strain. He could remember nothing except that he had been deplorably outspoken.

"Well, Vicar," said Dr. Robbertson, heartlessly jovial, "I dare say you can cross the Deanery of Wroxminster off your list of possible preferments."

"Glngk!"

"What's that, Vicar?"

"I—I feel suddenly unwell, Doctor. This—this—ah, *unavoidable* accident has taken more out of me than I had thought. I hope you'll excuse me."

Before the doctor could twist his knife any further, the vicar had rung off. Dr. Robbertson turned to the two young men.

"That's done it!" he exclaimed. "Dirk, you're superb!

First Lady Mauley and now this! When this gets around, you'll be the most popular chap in the parish!"

"He *is* an awful ass, isn't he?" said Dirk. "If he hadn't been so much older than me, I'd've knocked him down, the bloody fool!"

"You *have* knocked him down—in more ways than one! You have no idea!"

Tommy was smiling at them rather uncomprehendingly. The doctor recollected that his nephew probably knew nothing of the relationship of vicar and bishop.

"It's like this, Tommy . . ." he began.

Miss Granby had just finished a late lunch when Boudicca called her to the telephone.

"This is Stephen Robbertson, Miss Granby."

"Oh, hello, Doctor. I saw Lady Mauley in church this morning. She looked none the worse for her adventure of Saturday."

Dr. Robbertson laughed.

"I'm sure of it," he said. Then he added, "I was about to ring you a few minutes ago when—but I'll keep that until I see you, Miss Granby. Anyhow, I wondered if we might arrange a meeting tomorrow morning, either here or at your house? I think you wanted to discuss Hopkins?"

"Why, yes. I must confess that I'm simply bewildered by his poems. I'm sure they must mean *something,* but *what?*"

"That's not an unusual reaction. I think I've read 'The Windhover' a hundred times, and I'm still not at all sure I understand anything about it."

"Why don't you come here, Doctor? I'll have—Boudicca—make some coffee, and we can have a comfortable chat."

"Splendid!"

"Did—was there something else? You started to say . . ." Miss Granby paused.

"Well, there *is* something else. Henderson has had an adventure himself. Another goal in the Henderson–Cherton match, as it were."

"Oh, Dr. Robbertson, please don't keep me in suspense!"

Briefly, he described the morning's accident, appending to his account a verbatim report of his recent conversation with Mr. Staine.

Presently Miss Granby went to the kitchen, trying to regain her composure.

"Dr. Robbertson is coming over for coffee tomorrow morning. Will you make some of those little cakes with the lemon zest and currants, please?"

Dr. Robbertson had just settled down with his sketching pad and charcoal when the telephone rang.

"Busy little machine," he muttered as Tommy answered it.

" 'Sfa you."

"Doctor? This is Emily Mauley. I'm just calling to remind Mr. Henderson to bring his—ah—his Vespa. The bishop *must* try it!"

"Of course, Lady Mauley. We'd not forgotten." He paused. "Lady Mauley?"

"Yes, Doctor?"

"You remember Miss Granby, don't you?"

"Fanny? Of course. I caught a glimpse of her at the funeral this morning, but there was such a crush that she got away before I could speak to her. I wanted to ask her to join us this afternoon. What about her, Doctor?"

"Why, just that, Lady Mauley. Miss Granby is quite an admirer of yours, and I was going to take the liberty of suggesting that she might like to see you."

"Umgh! . . . Well, I shall telephone her immediately. About four o'clock? Splendid! *Good*-bye, Doctor."

The day had continued clear and sunny, and by midafternoon it was quite warm. Birkett was supervising the arrangement of chairs and umbrellas on the terrace overlooking the East Parterre and the folly when Lady Mauley appeared with Miss Pollock.

"Very nice, Birkett," said Lady Mauley approvingly. "Everyone should be quite comfortable."

Miss Pollock doubted that everyone was going to be quite comfortable, but she knew better than to say so. At least the Staines and the Hitchcocks would not be present. She wondered whether she had time to make herself a martini before the festive throng arrived. She looked at her watch and decided that she had.

"Where're *you* going?"

"To the dining room, Cousin Emily," said Miss Pollock with dignity.

"Well, Agnes, bring me one, too, please—with plenty of ice."

Miss Pollock laughed and entered the house.

Lady Mauley considered.

"I wonder if we should really bother about tea. That young American won't want it, I'm sure. Still, someone may, so perhaps we'd better have it, Birkett."

"Yes, m'lady."

"Now—well, I think you can put the bar over *there,* in the shade of that larch. Be sure that there's enough ice. And"—Lady Mauley dropped her voice—"you have that little flask I gave you, Birkett?"

"Yes, m'lady," said Birkett grimly. "I shall follow your instructions."

"And be sure that you use the vodka that the grand duke sent to Lord Mauley."

"Yes, m'lady. Er—it's extremely strong, m'lady."

"I know, Birkett," said Lady Mauley with a faint smile.

"Julia! So nice to see you again! Wasn't last night delightful?"

Mrs. Dodridge agreed that it was.

"Where's Thelma?" asked Lady Mauley.

"She's coming with Charles. He drove her into the village to post a parcel."

"And those two pleasant young men?"

"I really don't know, Lady Mauley. I dare say they'll be here shortly. Yes, I think I hear the Vespa now."

Down the avenue, traveling at a most sedate pace, came Dirk and Tommy. Both were wearing dark suits, white shirts, and conservative ties. Mrs. Dodridge was astonished to see how very presentable the pair could look. (Although she could not condone Tommy's hair, she admired it.)

Lady Mauley waved her stick as the Vespa slowed to a stop.

"Just leave it there at the foot of the steps, Mr. Henderson."

The youths dismounted and smiled at Lady Mauley as they came up the steps.

"I'm pleased to see you and Mr. Corelli. You've met Mrs. Dodridge. Where's your uncle, Mr. Corelli?"

"He's gone ta pick up Miss Granby. He oughta be here in a minute, ma'am," said Tommy, bowing to Mrs. Dodridge and Miss Pollock.

"Splendid! Now let's all sit down and *enjoy* ourselves! I see no real need to wait for the others."

Lady Mauley seated herself behind the tea tray but gestured toward the bar.

"I know I asked you for tea," she said, "but there are more stimulating arrangements over there, which cheer *and* inebriate. You will, of course, have cocktails if you prefer them."

Tommy's eyes lighted up and he glanced at Dirk, who gave him a discreet wink.

"What would *you* like, Julia?"

"A vodka martini," said Mrs. Dodridge with decisive abandon.

"I'm so glad you've taken the initiative, Julia," said the hostess. She looked around with a menacing smile. "Does *anyone* want tea? I know *you* don't, Agnes. You've already decided."

No one wanted tea.

"Ah, here're the bishop and Thelma!" exclaimed Lady Mauley. "And Miss Granby and Dr. Robbertson with them!"

The quartet descended from the car and mounted the terrace steps. Miss Granby was startled by the transformation in the two young men. If they weren't exactly Savile Row, they were a long way from the East End. (There was definitely an Italian accent to Tommy's beautifully cut suit.) Civilities were exchanged.

"Miss Granby! I'm happy you could come," said Lady Mauley.

"Thank you, Lady Mauley. I hope Lord Mauley is improving?"

"Oh, he's getting along nicely, thank you. It's unfortunate he can't join us today, but the doctor insists that he stop in bed for a day or two more."

Those who thought it necessary showed a decent sympathy, but Lady Mauley cut short the kind wishes by a renewal of her offer of tea or cocktails or both.

Birkett, presiding at the bar, relied upon thirty years of discipline to keep his face impassive, but his self-command was severely taxed by the time Dr. Robbertson had reached the history of his conversation with the vicar. The doctor had a talent for mimicry, and it was not in Birkett's imagination alone that there was a vivid picture of the Vicar of St. Margaret's in the grip of shock.

"Dear me!" said the bishop ruefully, trying to regain some vestige of episcopal dignity. "I shouldn't laugh, but—"

"Why on earth not, Charles?" asked Mrs. Dodridge. "I just wish I had seen it!"

"I wish *I* had!" exclaimed Dr. Robbertson and Miss Granby in unison. They smiled at each other.

"Oh, now you must enjoy yourselves!" said Lady Mauley. "Here, Mr. Henderson, I'm sure you'd like that refreshed! Birkett? Please see to Mr. Henderson's glass—and the bishop's."

"Oh, thank you, Lady Mauley," said the bishop, "but one is quite enough."

"Nonsense, Bishop! I never heard of such a thing! You deserve an ambrosial reward for your contribution. Birkett, fill the bishop's glass!"

Lady Mauley waited for a pause and then collected eyes. *"Now,"* she said, "Mr. Henderson, I want you to show the bishop how to ride that fascinating machine down there!"

The bishop opened his mouth to protest but his sister-in-law cut in.

"Charles, you know you'd love it!" (The bishop knew no such thing.) "Mr. Henderson, please show him how it works."

Lady Thelma muttered something. As she was sitting next to him, the bishop could catch the last of it: "'. . . and is marvelous in our eyes.'"

Dirk rose to his feet. As he did so, he wondered how Birkett was making the drinks. Dirk knew that he had a strong head; surely two drinks shouldn't affect him like this! And *why* should they taste of licorice? "C'mon, sir," he said with an amiable grin. "It's easy to drive—a real vintage number!"

The bishop, defeated, went carefully down the steps, puzzled as to how the control of circumstances had so completely eluded him.

Although rather sore from his morning's experience, the vicar felt that he really owed it to Lord Mauley's goodwill to pay him a visit. He had not been at the Hall since Saturday morning, and it was now Monday afternoon. As he cycled down the Hall drive, he decided that his stiff legs would benefit by additional exercise, so he turned into a side path that led to the central alley of the park. There was a slight declivity, and, after getting up fair speed, the vicar ceased to pedal and enjoyed coasting down the smooth gravel path to the intersection with the broader alley at its foot. At that moment, he heard the abominable sound of a motorbicycle, but he concluded that it must be on the main road. Certainly there would be no motorbicycle in Mauley Park!

But there was. At the moment at which the vicar reached the alley, the bishop reached the side path leading into it. The bishop had attained a speed of some forty m.p.h.; there was a ditch to his right and the vicar to his left. His only possible choice was to keep going, and this he did. The vicar instinctively clamped down upon both brakes; his bicycle skidded in the gravel and then catapulted its rider into the ditch on the opposite side of the road, where, after a moment's wobbling indecision, it joined him.

Only Mr. Staine's feet were visible above the level of the ditch, and in the distance could be heard the decreasing roar of the Vespa. Dirk had shown the bishop how to start the machine. If the young man had told him how to stop it, the bishop had forgotten.

"Bishop mus' be takin' th' long way roun' th' park," said Dr. Robbertson.

Mrs. Dodridge was a little concerned.

"Surely he should be back by now," she said, suppressing a hiccup.

" 'Sgreat li'l bike!" said Dirk proudly.

"Bishop's great guy," said Dr. Robbertson, nodding cordially to Birkett.

"'He hath put up with thoth of low degree an' exalted down th' seats of th' mighty,'" remarked Lady Thelma as she smiled benignly at Tommy. She looked about. "Whooo s-said that? Milt'n? Ar'stoll?"

"Iss th' 'Te Deum.'" volunteered Miss Granby. (What was happening to her tongue, she wondered.) Then she amended her remark. "No. 'S 'Mag'—'s 'Mag-niffy-cat,'" she said carefully.

"Tedium?" asked Lady Thelma, puzzled. Then she smiled again at Tommy. "D'ya know what a pre—pretty young man y'are?" she asked.

"Yeh," said Tommy, returning her smile and pressing his leg close against Dirk's.

Dirk considered Tommy disapprovingly. "Nau—naughty! Not *now,* ya silly twit!" he whispered.

"*Here* comes th' bishop!" cried Miss Pollock gaily. She waved her half-empty glass above her head, and the contents splashed over Lady Mauley. Birkett moved forward to mop.

"Never mind, Birkett," said Lady Mauley. "It's an old dress."

" 'San ol', ol' dress," chortled Miss Pollock, holding out her glass. " 'Nother, please."

The bishop speeded toward the terrace. As he reached the foot, he swerved away and began to circle the sundial on the parterre. The group above him watched, fascinated, as the bishop proceeded to ride round and round the sundial. Above the roar, he could be heard shouting, but no one could understand what he was trying to convey. He freed one hand for a momentary gesture of wild desperation, grabbed the handlegrip again, and whizzed off down the avenue and out of sight.

"Christ!" exclaimed Tommy. "He reely likes it!" He looked cheerfully toward the bar. "Where's Bir—Bir—where'za buttlerer? I'm thirzday."

" 'S Monday," whispered Dirk. "I wanna drink—where *is* good ol' Birkett?"

Birkett had retreated through the French windows to the drawing room.

The Second Coming was rather less spectacular. The Vespa was sputtering. The bishop had not made more than two circuits of the sundial when the machine coughed, slowed down, gave another cough, and came to a stop. He sat for a moment with bowed head. Then he dismounted carefully, gave the standard a vicious kick, and shakily crossed to the terrace steps.

"Bravo!" shouted Lady Thelma, applauding with a singular lack of coordination.

Dirk was enthusiastic.

"Didja run outa petrol, Bish?" he asked as the bishop gained the terrace. "I'm sorry. I shoulda filled 'er up. Howja like it? Fun, huh?"

The bishop stared bleakly at the grinning Dirk. The youth's soused good nature was infectious. It was impossible for the bishop to restrain a smile, in spite of the state of his nerves and buttocks.

"A—a most interesting—experience," he said, expelling his breath. "I should like to have a drink."

Mrs. Dodridge chuckled inanely from her chair.

" 'S *all* ya' need, Charlie boy!"

"Julia!"

"Mmm? Yesss?" asked Mrs. Dodridge vaguely.

"Oh, nothing. Ah, thank you, Birkett."

The bishop looked at the others. Dr. Robbertson was apparently asleep. Tommy had one arm around Dirk and the other around Miss Granby, who was, it seemed, reciting poetry under her breath. Miss Pollock and Lady Thelma were trying to touch glasses for a toast to the Vespa, but each was missing the other's glass by a good foot. Lady Mauley, seated with her hands folded upon the head of her stick, surveyed with serene content the deteriorating social fabric. Presently, she nodded and appeared to doze.

The bishop sat down and tried to frame in his mind his forthcoming interview with the vicar. His mind, however, refused to have any part of such a scheme. Gloomily he looked about. The sun was very low, yet no one seemed to have any idea that he would do anything but sit on the terrace all night.

The bishop rose, glanced at his somnolent hostess, and motioned to Birkett to follow him. In the shelter of the drawing room window, the bishop gave a brief nod toward the debauchees on the terrace.

"I—I really think, Birkett, that we should try to get these people home."

"Yes, my lord."

The bishop eyed the butler.

"What *did* you put in those drinks, Birkett?"

Birkett flushed.

"I—I was instructed to make them strong, my lord—and Lady Mauley asked me to use a special liqueur her ladyship provided."

The bishop raised his eyebrows, and Birkett's color deepened.

"You can tell me, Birkett. I'll regard it as a confidence," said the bishop.

"I—I don't know what it was, my lord. Absinthe is supposed to have that—effect, but I believe that's not really so. Perhaps it was a mild narcotic, sir?"

"Oh, I hardly think so," said the bishop. He looked toward the terrace again and shook his head. "Well, I think I shall quietly return to Mrs. Dodridge's house. I shall go out by the front door and leave my car here. I—I'm afraid it's useless to try to arouse the others."

"Perhaps so, my lord."

"It has been quite an afternoon, Birkett!" said the bishop as they walked to the front entrance.

"It has indeed, my lord," said Birkett, trying to suppress a treacherous twitch that threatened his mouth.

As they reached the door, the bishop took out his pocket book.

"Here, Birkett. With my thanks!"

"My lord?"

"Go on—take it. I couldn't have had an afternoon like this for ten pounds anywhere else in the world."

The bishop grinned and placed a finger on his lips. Then he winked and set out down the drive into the gathering dusk.

19

"Well, Lela, dear," said Mrs. Hitchcock, looking at the clock, "I really must be getting back. Thomas has gone to Porford for a meeting, but Félicité will be wondering what's become of me."

"I'm sorry you missed Frederick. He certainly should have returned by now. He's not usually this long at the Hall."

"It's still quite light, isn't it? Not long before summer will be with us again," said Mrs. Hitchcock, rising.

Mrs. Staine saw her to the door. As she opened it, she was

startled to see her husband, haggard and mud-encrusted, standing on the steps.

"Frederick! What on *earth!"*

"Why, Vicar! Did you have *another* fall?"

Mr. Staine glowered at the two women, muttered "Abominable!" and disappeared up the staircase.

Mrs. Hitchcock stared at Mrs. Staine.

"What—"

"I—I don't *know!* I *told* you about this morning, but—"

"Can it have happened *again?*"

"Hardly! Well, Portia, I *really* must excuse myself, *if* you'll forgive me? I'd better see to Frederick."

"Oh, of course! Of *course! Do* let me know if there's *anything* we can do!"

Mrs. Staine shut the door behind her guest and went cautiously up the stairs to the bathroom, from which imprecations could be heard.

"Frederick?"

"Don't speak to me, Lela!" said the vicar, glaring at his wife.

"But I *must* speak to you, dear! What on *earth* is the matter?"

"The matter is that Cherton is peopled with irresponsible lunatics! I was nearly killed by some fool on a motor-bicycle!"

"Oh, *not* the same man!"

"It might just as well've been," snarled the vicar, "but it wasn't. No, I do *not* know who it was! I had no time to see!"

He described his mishap, his voice partly muffled in a towel.

"In Mauley Park?" asked his wife.

"Didn't I *say* it was in Mauley Park?" he snapped.

"But—who—"

"If I knew, woman, I'd bring action! Don't think that I shan't complain to Lord Mauley! And in the strongest possible terms!"

Simms appeared. Her eyes rounded as she saw her employer, but she merely said, "The Bishop of Wroxminster is on the telephone, sir. His lordship would like to speak to you."

The vicar shuddered. Then he tried to rally.

"I'll come at once," he said, very nearly inaudibly.

He limped down the stairs and picked up the telephone hopelessly.

"This is Charles Dodridge, Vicar. I'm calling to ask how you are. I'm terribly distressed by this accident."

"Oh, thank you, Bishop. I—I'm really quite well. A—a bit shaken up, you know, but"—he laughed hollowly and unconvincingly—"these little, ah, upsets happen to everyone, you know."

"I feel extremely concerned, Vicar. I was driving—"

Mr. Staine interrupted with assurances as frantic as they were heartfelt.

"Oh, it was really nothing, nothing at all, Bishop. I—I had a good lunch and was soon as fit as a fiddle." Here the vicar laughed again.

The bishop suddenly realized that the vicar was speaking exclusively of the morning's accident. Life seemed brighter. He decided to let sleeping dogs lie.

"Well, Vicar, I'm relieved to learn that you're all right. Take care of yourself. How is Mrs. Staine?"

The bishop rang off, and the vicar returned to his ablutions.

The bishop sat down to dinner alone, wondering when, and in what condition, his sister-in-law would return.

It was past nine o'clock when Mrs. Dodridge arrived.

"Are you all right, Julia?"

"Oh, *Charles!*"

The bishop grinned. Mrs. Dodridge sank into an armchair.

"*What* an afternoon!" she exclaimed. "I'm ashamed of myself!"

"You had plenty of company, Julia," said the bishop, trying not to laugh. "You and Thelma were two of the most amusing creatures I've seen in a long time."

"Oh, Charles!"

"How do you feel?"

"Perfectly ghastly! And Thelma's the same! *What* an experience!"

"Those were quite strong drinks."

"Strong! They were poison!"

"Is everyone safely home now?"

"I hope so, Charles. After we had supper, Birkett had Cartwright drive Thelma, Fanny, Robbie, and those two boys—in your car. It's here, I see. *I* walked. I felt I needed it! That blessed Vespa is dead at the sundial."

"Where was Lady Mauley? Was she still asleep?"

"Lady Mauley! Hah! She ordered supper and gallons of strong coffee and made conversation until I thought I'd go mad. Then she retired. She was as bright as a button. Poor Agnes Pollock had to be carried to bed by the housekeeper and one of the maids! And *then*—in the middle of supper—those two young men started to— Heaven knows what poor Birkett thought!"

"Oh, dear! And what was Dr. Robbertson doing?"

"How I wish I knew! He disappeared into the library with Fanny Granby and was gone for what seemed hours! As for *Thelma*— But no. I'll keep that to myself."

"Well!" the bishop exclaimed. "Perhaps I left too soon."

"*No* one left too soon, *believe* me, Charles!"

"Oh, now come, Julia! What has become of your sense of humor? Really!"

Mrs. Dodridge considered. Then she managed a slight laugh.

"Yes. Yes, I suppose I shall look at it with a less jaundiced eye in the morning. . . . Oh, did you have a good dinner? Has Edwards looked after you?"

"I had an excellent dinner and some of James's famous port."

"I'm so glad. What a harrowing experience *you* had! Why *did* you keep riding that machine for so long?"

The bishop explained. Then he added, "It was unnerving at the time, but in retrospect it seems quite enjoyable—certain aspects particularly."

"In—retrospect," said Mrs. Dodridge slowly. "That reminds me of something Thelma said the other day. Perhaps Cherton must be lived in retrospect. Perhaps then it really *is*, well, amusing—if not enjoyable."

"You mustn't get up for me in the morning. I shall have to be off early. I'll be back for tea, I think."

"Oh, I shall be all right in the morning. Indeed, I'm much better already. I drank quantities of coffee and ate the richest things I could see—and my walk helped. *What* an afternoon!"

"So you've already said."

"Yes, Charles, but no matter how often I say it, I still can't quite believe it. And those two young men!"

"Now, Julia, for goodness sake! You must have known what they're like. I thought their behavior was exemplary, although young Corelli was a little overly demonstrative."

"Demonstrative! You weren't at the supper party! I'm willing to be as broad-minded and tolerant as the next, Charles, even to thinking that Corelli's hair is exquisite, but—"

The bishop shook his head in mild reproof.

"That 'but,' my dear Julia," he said, "comprises all of your prejudices. Don't worry about the young men. I've had a good deal of experience, my dear, and that they are able to be so well-mannered, so considerate of others—look at Henderson's kindness to Lady Mauley and to me—and as good-humored as they are says a lot for their basic qualities. Believe me, Julia, I've some idea of what both have probably endured before attaining peace of mind. Don't offer them sanctimonious pity; just treat them as fellow human beings who happen to be a bit different in one respect. They were drunk—*in vino veritas*, and"—the bishop smiled—"at least they weren't vindictive or belligerent in their cups. They've adjusted well, I think."

Mrs. Dodridge was trying to adjust her ideas and said nothing.

"Well," continued the bishop, "I didn't intend to give you a sermon, dear Julia, but just remember that you must learn to make sure that your theories of tolerance and so on can withstand the onslaught of reality."

"I think I see what you mean, Charles," said Mrs. Dodridge slowly. "I'll try. And they *are* charming—and evidently very fond of one another." She laughed. "*Very* evidently!"

20

Dirk carried Tommy into Dr. Robbertson's sitting room and gently placed him on the sofa. Tommy opened his eyes and looked up with a little smile.

"Where's Robbie?" he asked.

"He got out of the car with Miss Granby. Guess he'll be here after a while."

"Dirk, I wanna go ta bed. I'm still stoned."

"All right, sweetie. Want me to help you?"

"Yeh. You'll havta undress me. Ya mind?"

"*Mind!* Are you crackers?"

Dirk bent over and lifted the boy into his arms.

In the dim light of the pretty bedroom, Miss Granby sighed.

"Stephen!"

"My dear Fanny!"

"What time is it, Stephen?"

"Past three, darling."

"It doesn't seem possible. My dear!"

"Fanny!"

"You—you don't think less of me?"

"Of course I don't, silly! I think more of you. I wish this had happened sooner."

There was silence for a time.

"I've admired you for such a long while, Stephen."

"Have you, Fanny? I wish I'd known you better."

Miss Granby sighed again.

"I'm such a fraud, Stephen. All my silly little pretenses!"

"You're not pretending now, Fanny. You're such a dear."

"Hold me to you, Stephen. *Oooh!* That's so lovely!"

It was past dawn. Mrs. Staine came to with a start.

"Oh, Frederick! Not *again!*"

"Lela—dear."

"But I'm so *tired,* Frederick."

"Just—just once more? I'm quite unwell, my dear."

"*Unwell!* I'd hate to see you—oh, all right. Let's get it over with!"

"Thank you, my dear."

Miss Pollock opened her eyes, shuddered, and closed them again. She groped for the water carafe. After a few minutes, she despaired of further sleep without assistance. She groaned as she got out of bed and sought the bottle of sleeping tablets. The prescribed dose was one every six hours. She groaned again and took three tablets. Then she staggered back to bed.

In the adjoining room, Lady Mauley snored peacefully as her maid came in with the early tea. The girl softly placed the tray upon the bedside table and then drew back the window curtains. Lady Mauley opened her eyes, one at a time.

"*Good* morning, Brett! What time is it?"

"Half-past seven, m'lady."

"Is Miss Pollock up?"

"No, ma'am. Miss Pollock's still asleep. Shall I call her, m'lady?"

"Heavens no! Let the poor soul sleep. Bring me some wheat biscuits, Brett. I'm famished!"

"Yes, m'lady."

21

Thomas Hitchcock entered the breakfast parlor with a dignity that would have been excessive in a Flamen of Jupiter. His wife acknowledged his presence with a stately nod.

"Good morning, Thomas."

"Ah—yes," said Mr. Hitchcock, seating himself.

"You came in late?" hazarded his wife.

"I returned at approximately twelve o'clock, Portia," said Mr. Hitchcock. He frowned as he looked at the table. "Kippers?"

"I didn't hear you."

"I merely remarked 'kippers,' Portia."

"Yes, they are, aren't they?"

"Presumably."

"I didn't hear you come in. I must have been sleeping quite soundly."

Mrs. Hitchcock poured a cup of tea for her husband.

"How was the meeting?" she asked.

Mr. Hitchcock sampled a kipper before replying.

"Excellent," he said.

"Was it really?"

"No, it was interminable. The kipper, I mean."

"An interminable kipper, Thomas? I don't understand."

"Obviously. No, the *meeting* was interminable."

"How tiresome," said Mrs. Hitchcock sympathetically.

"Sir Henry went on and on about that absurd book of his."

"Is it to be published?"

"I certainly trust not. Really, Portia, what can you do with a man who insists that Jane Austen was the natural daughter of the Prince Regent?"

Mrs. Hitchcock stared.

"Eh?" she said.

"Sir Henry has found a cryptogram, he says," said Mr. Hitchcock, stirring his tea.

"A cryptogram, Thomas? Where?"

"In the dedication of *Emma.*"

"How extraordinary!" remarked Mrs. Hitchcock.

"The man's a fool," said her husband.

"Oh, Thomas! That reminds me! The vicar?"

"What about him?"

"He had an accident yesterday morning. After you left yesterday, I stopped to chat with Lela. She said—"

Mr. Hitchcock indulged in a tolerant smile.

"I know about it," he said. "Hoare told me when I stopped off for a pint on the way to Porford."

"Yes, but—but it happened *again! Something* happened, anyhow!" said Mrs. Hitchcock and described her encounter with the vicar. "He was evidently *very* disturbed," she added.

"It sounds as if it *had* happened again, Portia. But he had reason enough to be disturbed by the fracas yesterday morning. He never has got along with the bishop, you know."

"The *bishop,* Thomas? What has the bishop to do with it?"

"Didn't Lela tell you? No, I suppose she wouldn't."

"Thomas, *do* tell me!"

He told her.

"And Mr. Staine never knew it at the time?" she asked in wonder.

"Hoare said not."

"How did Hoare hear of it?"

"I don't really know, my dear Portia. Perhaps through his daughter. That girl keeps her ears open, you know."

"Boudicca?"

"Umm."

Mrs. Hitchcock examined her plate. Then she helped herself to more jam, poured another cup of tea, and pondered. Her husband fed in comparative silence.

"It's strange that we didn't know the bishop was here," she said presently.

"Why so? We scarcely know him."

"No, but we're such a small place. You'd think that *someone*—"

"He is staying with Julia Dodridge, Portia," said Mr. Hitchcock pointedly.

"Oh—of course."

Mrs. Hitchcock felt unequal to further comment. It was sufficiently annoying that Mrs. Dodridge's brother-in-law was a bishop. That her brother was a duke, she preferred to ignore whenever possible.

"Do—do you think we should call?"

"On the bishop?"

"No, Thomas. On the Staines."

Mr. Hitchcock frowned judicially. His wife could not determine whether he was weighing her suggestion or trying to decide between peach marmalade and gooseberry jam.

"I should *like* to," he said finally, "but perhaps it would be kinder—just now—*not* to."

"Mmm—yes, perhaps so."

Mrs. Hitchcock buttered a piece of toast, looked at the result, and slowly bit it as if she thought it might bite back.

"Don't you think it rather odd that we've not seen Lady Mauley?"

"We spoke to her at the funeral yesterday, Portia."

"Yes, but—well, I know that we don't know her at all well, but we *do* know Lord Mauley."

"Perhaps," said Mr. Hitchcock acidly, "*that* is precisely why we don't know *her!*"

"Lady Mauley *can* be quite trying, of course," said Mrs. Hitchcock cautiously.

"Umm."

"Well, I must talk to Félicité about dinner. Will veal cutlets and a salad do for lunch, Thomas?"

"Umm."

"I *must* see to those hyacinths, too. Are you going out this morning?"

"I thought I might stroll down to the Rose after I've

worked a bit on *Cranford*. What was Fanny doing up so late, I wonder?"

"Fanny?"

"There were lights in her house when I came in at midnight."

"Perhaps she hadn't gone to bed."

"That is a not unreasonable surmise, Portia."

"Well, I must speak to Félicité," she said, rising.

"Interminable," muttered her husband, staring at the kippers.

22

It was nearly eleven o'clock in the morning when Philip Tunstall turned in at the Hall gates and drove up the avenue to the rambling old house.

His wife drew a deep breath before saying, "All right, Philip. I played Lady Bountiful to your precious Evanses. The least you can do for me is to try and be decently civil to Charlie."

"I'm *here*, Jean. I shall treat your brother with all the consideration of which I think him worthy."

"That is by no means enough, and—good heavens! That's Mother on the terrace!"

Mr. Tunstall brightened.

"I believe you're right. Well!"

As they approached, Lady Mauley waved at them and began to walk down the steps.

"Mother! How long have you been here?"

"*Centuries*, Jean! Hello, Philip. It's good to see you again, my dear. Agnes will be glad that you've come. She's a little unwell this morning, but nothing serious."

Mr. Tunstall bent to give Lady Mauley a filial kiss.

"How's Charlie?" he asked, trying to sound as if he cared.

"Oh, he's all right. He's getting up this morning," said Lady Mauley.

"Has he been in bed all this time?" asked her daughter.

Mr. Tunstall interrupted.

"What is *that* thing doing there?" he asked, pointing to the Vespa, over which Birkett had draped a plastic sheet.

"Oh!" exclaimed Lady Mauley. "A most interesting vehicle. You should have seen the bishop riding about on it yesterday!"

"The bishop?" asked Mr. Tunstall incredulously.

Mrs. Tunstall was suspicious.

"Mother, what have you been up to?"

"Oh, nothing, my dear Jean," said Lady Mauley airily. "I asked a few people over for tea yesterday. I felt that Cherton needed a bit of—of *loosening up,* as it were."

"And was Bishop Dodridge's careering about on that thing a part of the—*déclenchement?*" asked Mr. Tunstall.

Lady Mauley grinned.

"The bishop added a good deal to the gaiety of the afternoon, even if he did see fit to take French leave."

"I don't blame him in the least," said Mrs. Tunstall, shaking her head. "Really, Mother, you're irrepressible!"

"Umgh! How long will you both be here?"

The Tunstalls and Lady Mauley were enjoying a prelunch glass of sherry when Philip Tunstall's attention was diverted by something beyond the drawing room windows.

"Who's that chap pouring petrol into the Vespa?" he asked. "Is he a new servant?"

Lady Mauley stood up to look.

"Oh! That's the delightful young man who brought me to Cherton on the Vespa!"

"What?" Mr. Tunstall almost yelled.

"Mother!"

"Yes, indeed. A charming young friend of Dr. Robbertson's, a model, I believe. His name is Henderson. You *must* meet him!"

"One of Robbie's—" began Mrs. Tunstall in astonishment, but Lady Mauley was already calling from one of the French windows.

"Yoo hoo! Mr. Henderson! *Good* morning! Just come in here a moment, young man. I want you to meet someone."

Dirk looked startled and pushed back the hair falling over his forehead. Then he smiled, replaced the cover of the fuel tank, and made his way to the drawing room.

"Good morning, ma'am," he said. His leather jacket, boots, and scarlet open-neck shirt might have worried him in other circumstances, but for some time he had ceased to worry about any circumstances involving Lady Mauley.

Lady Mauley made the necessary introductions, then signed to her son-in-law to pour a glass of sherry for Dirk.

Mrs. Tunstall looked furtively at her husband, who was making polite conversation with the young man. Philip Tunstall appeared to be in an exceptionally sunny mood. In fact, he seemed to be trying hard not to smile too broadly.

Lady Mauley related recent events, but she left to Dirk the now-famous encounter with the vicar; neither mentioned the party.

When Mrs. Tunstall could command herself, she looked at her mother and said, "What a pity you can't be in Cherton all the time!"

"Jean, I consider that a suggestion that borders on the psychopathic in its morbidity. Live in Cherton, indeed!"

"Really, Lady Mauley," said Mr. Tunstall, "I feel that you're keeping something back, you know."

"So do I. Mother, what happened at that little gathering yesterday afternoon?"

Birkett, who was serving cheese pastries, nearly dropped the plate he was proffering to Lady Mauley. She gave him a diabolical look and then smiled beatifically at her daughter. Birkett left, sighing. Dirk was absorbed in this view of the upper classes at home.

"Why, nothing, really, my dear Jean. Oh, perhaps one or two rather overextended themselves with the vodka—"

"Vodka?" asked Mr. Tunstall. He repeated his wife's

earlier question: "Lady Mauley, what *have* you been up to?"

Lady Mauley turned and smiled at Dirk. Then she suddenly folded her hands sedately in her lap, lowered her eyes, and said nothing.

"Le déclenchement du village," muttered Mrs. Tunstall sotto voce.

Seeing his mother-in-law had resolved to be uncommunicative, Mr. Tunstall turned to Dirk. "So you like Cherton, Mr. Henderson?" he asked.

"Yes, sir, I do. I've had a hell of—I mean, I've had a very good time here." He smiled at his hostess. "Lady Mauley has been awfully nice to me—and to Tommy, too, ma'am," he added.

"Oh!" exclaimed Lady Mauley. "That handsome young American! Where is Mr. Corelli this morning? What is *he* doing?"

When Dirk left the house, Tommy had been amusing himself by sliding naked down the greased bannisters.

"He—he was playing a sort of game when I left, ma'am," he said.

"A game? A card game?" asked Lady Mauley.

"No, ma'am. With—uh—balls."

"Well, you must bring him here before I leave. I should like to see a great deal more of him."

Dirk fought to repress the observation that was she to go to the doctor's immediately, she might well see all of Tommy. Then he finished his sherry and rose to leave, terrified lest his sense of humor lead him to some horrible gaffe.

They watched him mount the Vespa and drive slowly away. Mrs. Tunstall shook her head.

"Really, Mother, do you know what you're doing?"

Lady Mauley eyed her daughter with dignity.

"Don't I *usually* know what I'm doing, Jean?"

"Well, yes, but—"

"I *like* Mr. Henderson. I *like* Mr. Corelli. I *also* happen to like Stephen Robbertson. He minds his own business—which is more than can be said for most of the people in this *trou.* Does that answer your question, Jean?''

''I suppose so.''

''Jolly good for you, Lady Mauley!'' said Mr. Tunstall. Then he excused himself and went into the entrance hall, looking for Birkett. The butler emerged from the dining room as Philip Tunstall shut the drawing room door.

''Birkett!''

''Yes, Mr. Tunstall?'' said Birkett, crossing to him. ''Can I do anything for you, sir?''

''I hope so. What, if you don't mind telling me, what precisely went on at that party yesterday afternoon?''

Birkett's impassivity was no match for his memories.

''Ah—yes, sir.''

''Well?''

''You—you really want me to tell you, sir?''

''Certainly. Why else should I ask you?''

Birkett drew a deep breath.

''Well, sir,'' he said.

Philip Tunstall grinned as he stood alone outside the drawing room door. He decided that he would prolong his stay until his mother-in-law's departure for Maulcaster.

23

''So that,'' said Dr. Robbertson as he sat beside Miss Granby on her chintz-covered sofa, ''is what *I* make of 'The Windhover.' As Lela Staine would inaptly remark, it has to be read with a fine-tooth comb.''

Miss Granby smiled at him.

''You know, I don't really care much now,'' she said.

''What do you mean, Fanny?''

"About Hopkins. Oh, he's interesting, of course, but—I—I'm afraid I was just using him as a stalking-horse."

Dr. Robbertson frowned and leaned forward.

"Do you mean—for *me?*" he asked sharply.

Miss Granby reddened.

"Oh, good heavens, *no!* No, I didn't mean *that,* Stephen! *Please* believe me!"

The doctor relaxed, and Miss Granby continued.

"No, Stephen. It's all part of what I told you—last night. My silly pretenses. I'm no more of an intellectual than, well, than the vicar."

He laughed.

"Well, at least *you* know it!" he said.

"There's no one here to whom I can talk, Stephen. At least, not until now. The Staines and the Hitchcocks are such bores—and Lady Thelma and Mrs. Dodridge make me uneasy. I'm sure they've always seen through me."

"My dear Fanny! You mustn't be so diffident. With all your good qualities, you shouldn't despair because you're not a genius, you know."

"I'm not despairing, Stephen," she said quietly. "I'm just rather disgusted with myself."

"Well, you can talk to me, can't you? As much as you like."

"I'm glad of that," she said, smiling.

Dr. Robbertson poured himself another cup of coffee and picked up a cake.

"I understand how you must feel at times," he said. "It's like being buried alive, isn't it?"

"Oh, Stephen! You don't know!"

"I think I do, Fanny. I miss having that sort of companionship, too, you know. Oh, the boys are amusing, of course. That's one of the chief reasons I like to have them about. I enjoy their blasé ignorance—although I'm quite aware that other reasons have been ascribed by our kindly local gossips. But even so, it becomes very tiresome keeping to their level. That's why I spend so much time away from Cherton."

Miss Granby frowned.

"I've heard that gossip, Stephen, and it infuriated me. *Whose* business is it except yours? I couldn't've cared less—except I was afraid I'd never have a chance with you."

"It's hard to realize I'm hearing this in Cherton, Fanny!"

Miss Granby pondered.

"Stephen," she said at last, "why do you live in Cherton at all?"

Dr. Robbertson laughed.

"I might ask you the same question," he said. Then he went on. "It's a quiet, pretty place, and I find that many of my neighbors do wonders for my self-esteem. After talking to the vicar (which is an experience I generally try to avoid) or to, say, Charlie Mauley, I feel like Newton and Plato rolled into one."

Miss Granby laughed in turn.

"I've often thought of selling this place and moving to London," she said, "but I've never been able to do it. Perhaps because my father bought it years ago for his retirement, perhaps for very much the same reasons that you remain here."

"Let's face it, Fanny. I'd impress no one in London, and your little foibles would go entirely unremarked. Isn't that true?"

"Yes," said Miss Granby, sighing, "I'm afraid it is." Then she chuckled. "After all, I don't think even London could surpass Cherton in some ways."

"Such as—?"

"Well—Lady Mauley, for instance."

They both laughed, and the doctor took Miss Granby's hand.

"Fanny, we owe Lady Mauley a good bit, you know. We—we'd not be sitting here if it weren't for her."

"No, I know it. Oh, Stephen, I *am* so glad!"

"So am I, my dear."

Presently the doctor rose to go. Before he opened the sitting room door, he kissed her.

"Why don't we, just the two of us, have dinner at Wroxley on Friday?"

"I'd love it—but what about your guests?"

"Dirk can cook their dinner. Neither knows that I know it, but, believe me, they're quite anxious for me to get out from under their feet as much as possible."

"You'll come to tea today, Stephen?"

"Of course. But we'd better not be too much together too quickly, you know."

Miss Granby nodded.

"I know Cherton. I'm all for the sexual revolution and women's rights, but my idealism doesn't extend to mounting the local guillotine, so to speak."

The doctor chuckled.

"Nor mine. What would scarcely raise an eyebrow in London or Stockholm would raise every roof in the village, I think."

They reached the front door, where Boudicca was polishing the knocker, a copy of Thackeray's Gruffanuff.

"Thank you so much, Miss Granby. I trust I'll see you soon?"

"Thank *you*, Doctor. Your explanation of the poem was *most* enlightening."

"The cakes were very good," said Miss Granby to Boudicca as Dr. Robbertson strode through the gate.

"Thank you, ma'am," said Boudicca demurely.

Miss Granby reentered the house, and Boudicca continued to polish.

"Wonder whether they'll live at his house or here," she remarked to Gruffanuff.

Dr. Robbertson was cleaning brushes in his studio when his nephew wandered in.

"Oh, hello, Tommy. Sit down. I want to talk to you about something. It won't take long. I'm going to Miss Granby's for tea."

"Okay."

The doctor placed the brushes in a jar, dried his hands, and took a chair facing Tommy's.

"I want to talk to you about what you're going to do in the future, Tommy."

Tommy frowned, and his uncle continued.

"You're welcome to stay here and consider it your home for as long as you like. You know that. But we've got to do something to prepare you for some kind of future. You ought to be in school right now."

"I could go t'a trade school, I s'pose," said the boy rather dubiously. "Well, I guess I could—mebbe," he added, thinking of more attractive possibilities. There were, after all, all sorts of trades—and trade.

"A trade school? To learn what, Tommy?"

"Oh, I s'pose—'bout cars—or somethin'," was the vague response.

"Dirk's father had a garage, you know. Have you been talking to Dirk?"

"Sorta, Robbie. He wants ta show me round London. He says he knows somebody there whut hires fashion models. Mebbe I'd like that—gettin' paid ta show off clo'es an' things. Dirk says th' guy's got lotsa kids my age on th' payroll."

Dr. Robbertson felt as if he had been hit on the head by a pile driver. Could—could Tommy *possibly* be as dense as his remark implied? He stared in consternation at his nephew. Tommy gave a wriggle. Then he smiled at his uncle.

"Robbie, I'm not *reely* dumb, ya know. Jus' young, like ya said."

Dr. Robbertson felt he had to answer something, so he said, "You get along well with Dirk, don't you?"

"I get along fine with Dirk!" Tommy exclaimed, his smile widening.

"He has many good qualities. Perhaps he's a little too fond of money, but that's not unusual. As far as I can tell, Tommy, he hasn't a malicious fiber in him, and he certainly isn't vain.

You know, Dirk can be extremely thoughtful and generous. I've been able to help him once or twice, and he's shown himself unfailingly grateful."

"He's been reel good ta me, Robbie. I like him a lot. Hell, Robbie, I *love* him!" Tommy exclaimed, fed up with pussyfooting.

"I know you do," said the doctor, smiling, "and, Tommy—that's nobody's business but yours and his. I hope only that you're not going to let yourself get hurt. You're—if you don't mind my saying it—you're too sweet and gentle a boy to get mixed up with anyone who's going to take advantage of your good nature. So—just be careful."

Tommy turned his head to stare out of the window.

"I can take care of myself, Robbie," he said softly. "In Syracuse, I figgered out a lot about people. Hadta. An' I—I don't think Dirk'd take advantage of me."

"Neither do I. But sometimes things don't work out the way you expect. Time changes people, and somebody else might not be so kind as Dirk. Do you understand what I mean, Tommy?"

"Yeh—I unnastan'. Mebbe a whole lot more'n ya think."

"So?" asked the doctor.

"Well, Mom allus said if ya borrow trouble, ya could havta pay it back with int'res'."

For a moment Dr. Robbertson drummed with his fingers on the arm of his chair, looking gravely at his nephew.

"Sometimes I think you're older than I am," he said.

Tommy rose and crossed to his uncle's chair. He smiled and kissed him affectionately on the forehead.

"You're a great guy, Robbie," he said. "Don't worry 'bout me."

Dr. Robbertson placed one hand on Tommy's and said, "I hope you'll fall on your feet."

"I hope ta hell I don't fall on my ass!"

Miss Granby and Dr. Robbertson were sitting on the sofa before the fire, enjoying the cheer of the softly lit room, contrasted as it was with the icy rain pouring in the gloom beyond the curtained windows.

After a pause, Miss Granby spoke in a hesitating manner.

"Stephen, dear?"

"Yes, Fanny?"

"Would you tell me something? I'm rather puzzled."

"I shall if I can. What is it?"

"Well—Stephen—earlier today you mentioned your paintings. Stephen, if you don't mind my asking, *why* do you paint all those male life studies?"

Dr. Robbertson laughed.

"Money," he said, "pure and simple. The financial aspect is an important one. You see, there are many artists specializing in the female nude but only a very few painting males—and most of them are hopeless. There's quite a demand for my sort of work, and my clients know that I consider their tastes their own business. A less important reason is that although my having the boys popping in and out of Cherton raises eyebrows, it's nothing to what I'd have to put up with if I had young women posing for me." The doctor paused to light a cigarette; then he continued. "Quite frankly, I really think that, sex aside, the male body is a esthetically more pleasing—in better proportion and more suited to art. You see, Fanny, so many artists can't distinguish between their artistic and their sexual impulses. Not many are so frank as Renoir, I think it was, who said that he painted women with his penis." Dr. Robbertson laughed again. "Don't think I haven't had some outraged and virtuously indignant rebuttals from my colleagues! But consider the number of statues of the male figure that the Greeks did compared with those they made of females."

"Oh, but—the *Greeks,* Stephen!"

Dr. Robbertson shrugged.

"Their definitions weren't so narrow—or clear-cut, if you prefer—as ours. Well, *I* can function in either direction. Most people could, you know, but many are so clever at concealing the truth from themselves that they'd rather die than admit the possibility of such a thing. Why not express a close relationship in sexual terms?"

Miss Granby nodded.

"I seldom sleep with one of my models because I prefer to keep my relationship with them on a professional plane, but I'd be a liar if I said that I never do."

Miss Granby swallowed. Then she managed a grin.

"Well, I did ask you, didn't I?"

"Yes, Fanny, you did."

"You're—you're not annoyed are you, Stephen?"

"My dearest Fanny, don't be ridiculous! You asked me to tell you, and so I did. The day that I can make more money painting girls is the day that my studio will look like the old Folies Bergère. Until then—well, I suppose that Dirk and the rest of them are assured of an income. And I'll also tell you *this:* I'd like to paint *you!*"

Miss Granby laughed and rumpled the doctor's hair.

"Lovely! As a companion piece to Tommy's portrait? You can hang us both in your drawing room. Think what it might do for the vicar's blood pressure!"

Dr. Robbertson only smiled, his mind occupied in considering a drastic step that it had just occurred to him to take.

24

"Hello, Dobbins. Is Lady Thelma here?"

"Good afternoon, Mrs. Dodridge. Lady Thelma's in the dining room."

"Well, you're having an early tea, Thelma. Are you going out?"

Lady Thelma stared haggardly at her friend.

"Tea? This is *breakfast!* I've been up for less than an hour."

Mrs. Dodridge laughed.

"I didn't telephone. I thought you might be sleeping. How do you feel?"

"Oh, Julia!"

"Like that, eh? Too bad. I seem to've got off more lightly."

"And you were there before I arrived," said Lady Thelma reproachfully.

"Not long enough to have had one of those lethal drinks, you know."

"Lethal! How right you are! Julia, what happened to everyone?"

"Everyone got regally drunk, my dear—except our hostess. Naturally, *she* was as lively as a kitten."

Lady Thelma sipped her coffee.

"Julia," she said impressively, "I think she did it deliberately."

"Possibly," said Mrs. Dodridge. "It would be just like her." She paused and smiled. "How much of the evening do you remember?"

"Less than I should and more than I want to," replied Lady Thelma gloomily.

"I don't suppose," said Mrs. Dodridge casually, "that you remember proposing to Tommy Corelli?"

"Julia! I *didn't!*"

"Oh, everyone was quite good-natured about it. *He* was most amiable—especially considering the intensity of your avowal."

"Julia, you're trying to upset me! You—you *are* joking, aren't you?"

Mrs. Dodridge laughed again as she shook her head.

"Don't worry," she said. "Lady Mauley had gone to bed. There was no one there but ourselves—and Birkett, of course."

"*Birkett!* Do you mean that I—that I made a fool of myself in front of the servants? Oh, how dreadful!"

"As I said, only Birkett was there. I'm quite certain that he sent away the other servants on purpose."

"Oh, my God!" groaned Lady Thelma.

"Oh, dear. I came to cheer you up, and I seem to have upset you."

"Upset me! Do you wonder?"

"Now, Thelma, no one will remember anything about it, I promise you."

"*You* do," said Lady Thelma, still more gloomily.

"You know I have a very high tolerance for alcohol. Those cocktails must have been undiluted, imported Russian vodka, although I *think* there was something else. And they went down like milk." She grinned in spite of her attempt at sympathy. "Besides, your little performance was overshadowed by what went on afterward."

Lady Thelma looked a little happier.

"What happened?"

"Dirk and Tommy—I *cannot* think of them as 'mister'—played a love scene straight out of Genet. By *that* time, Robbie had supported Fanny Granby to the library, and Agnes Pollock had been carried to bed. I don't think that either boy was aware that anyone else was there. And *I* wasn't for long! *That* was when Birkett brought in Cartwright and packed you all into Charles's car."

"My God! Oh! . . . Charles? Wasn't *he* there?"

"No, unfortunately. The coward sneaked out while we were still on the terrace, long before that unmemorable supper party began!"

"So," mused Lady Thelma, "we must hope that Birkett—and Cartwright—will be discreet."

"Yes," said Mrs. Dodridge with a sigh. "Birkett's a very sensible man."

"What an experience! I used to think that *I* was a very sensible woman."

"You are, Thelma. No one could have foreseen what happened. And I'm positive those cocktails were doctored in some way."

"They must've been. What an outrageous thing to do!"

"Do you remember coming home?" asked Mrs. Dodridge. "I walked, after I'd seen you delicately poured into the car."

"I remember nothing. For all I know, I may have danced up and down the High in my nightgown!"

"Except for your slight lapse with Tommy, you conducted yourself with complete decorum. You were even quoting Scripture at one point."

"I *was* drunk, wasn't I!"

"Yes," said Mrs. Dodridge, grinning.

"I wish you had a split lip, Julia!" said Lady Thelma viciously.

"My dear Thelma, this experience will keep me in laughter for days. Charles told me that my sense of humor would return in the morning, and it has."

"I don't suppose *you* did anything out of character?" asked Lady Thelma, looking wistful.

Mrs. Dodridge smiled.

"I—I have a hideous conviction that sometime in the course of the evening I recommended Fowler to Fanny—and told her why."

"Is *that* all?" asked Lady Thelma scornfully.

"It's all I can remember," said Mrs. Dodridge apologetically.

"Let's hope your memory is as bad as mine, Julia. You're sure you didn't do a fan dance on the table, or something like that?"

Mrs. Dodridge moved uneasily.

"Not that I know of," she said. Then she gasped. "Oh, *no!*" she exclaimed, putting her hands to her face, which had suddenly gone scarlet.

"What is it?"

"You—you don't remember? About—about the Chinese vase?"

"What Chinese vase?"

"Thank god!"

"Julia, what is it?"

Mrs. Dodridge groaned and closed her eyes, shaking her head.

"You will never, *never* know," she said.

"Was it something *I* did?"

Mrs. Dodridge continued to shake her head. Lady Thelma cheered up.

"Something *you* did, Julia?"

"Yes—I think so," muttered Mrs. Dodridge, shuddering.

"How do you feel now?" asked Lady Thelma.

"Perfectly dreadful!" said Mrs. Dodridge.

"*I* feel *much* better. *Sure* you won't tell me?"

"Absolutely certain, Thelma. If I had a confessor, I wouldn't tell *him!*"

"Well!" exclaimed Lady Thelma briskly. "It looks like it's going to be a lovely day, doesn't it?"

"Beastly," said her friend. "Let me have some of that coffee, will you, please?"

"Of course," said Lady Thelma, ringing for another cup.

After Dobbins had left, Mrs. Dodridge looked wanly at her hostess.

"Thelma, if it ever comes to light, I shall have to leave Cherton."

"Julia!"

"I mean it. My—my one chance is that it was a particularly vivid nightmare and not a memory."

"But what—well, never mind. Anyhow, I suppose we'll have to admit that life has been more interesting recently."

"Always retrospect! Once, just *once,* I should like to be conscious of enjoying myself at the time."

"Didn't you enjoy yourself yesterday?"

"I said *conscious* of enjoying myself, Thelma."

Lady Thelma considered.

"Why did Robbie and Fanny go into the library?"

"Why, indeed? *She* was reciting poetry most of the evening, and *he* kept telling her what a great writer Gerard Manley Hopkins was."

"Perhaps they wanted to read poetry together."

"That seems as reasonable as any other surmise."

"Or perhaps he felt neglected—with Dirk and Tommy er—carrying on like that."

"That, too, is possible."

"I seem to've missed a good deal," said Lady Thelma.

"For which we may both be thankful," said Mrs. Dodridge with another shudder.

"You think so, do you?"

"I *know* so," said Mrs. Dodridge firmly.

"Oh, I'd forgotten to mention it, but Dobbins tells me that Philip and Jean Tunstall arrived at the Hall this morning."

Mrs. Dodridge set down her cup with a crash.

"That *does* it!" she groaned. "Perfect! That's *all* we needed!"

"What do you mean, Julia?"

"Thelma, you know as well as I do that Philip Tunstall is as curious as a cat and has a tongue like a razor. If he hasn't already wormed the whole story out of Birkett, it's only because he hasn't yet thought of it—or hasn't yet heard of our genteel little orgy."

"But would he say anything, Julia?"

"He loathes Charlie Mauley, and he detests Cherton and all its quirks. This is *just* the sort of thing he'd *love* to broadcast to the winds of heaven!"

"Julia, for quiet sympathy and cheerful encouragement, you have no equal. *None!*"

"I'm sorry, dear, but we may as well be prepared for the worst. The only possible chance is that his devotion to Lady Mauley may keep him quiet."

"But he doesn't dislike you and me, Julia. At least, I don't think he does."

"No, he doesn't, but he loves a good story, and this one would be a godsend. *And* remember, he knows my brother. Edward may *be* thirty-two, but he has a teenager's sense of humor. Telling him all the dreadful details would be Philip's idea of heaven. Well, Thelma, *you* know what my darling little brother is like! Utterly enchantingly irresponsible—and a born raconteur." Suddenly Mrs. Dodridge gasped and went as white as she had previously been red.

"What now?" asked Lady Thelma nervously. "*Now* what've you thought of? What little pearl of consolation are you going to throw into my trough next?"

Mrs. Dodridge swallowed several times before she was able to speak.

"Edward is going to Windsor Castle in a fortnight. We—we may become notorious in rather exalted circles, Thelma!"

Lady Thelma stared.

"But, Julia! Surely—*surely* he wouldn't repeat it to the . . ." She paused, appalled.

Mrs. Dodridge shrugged.

"As you know, I've never met her, but I understand that she likes a joke as well as the next person. *This* would be *Edward's* idea of a joke!"

Lady Thelma looked listlessly hopeful.

"Maybe there'll be an atomic attack—or something," she said.

25

Miss Granby stared at Dr. Robbertson, her mouth frozen in a half-gasp, half-smile.

"Well, really, Fanny, you needn't look so astonished," said the doctor, smiling.

"I—Stephen—I don't know what to say," she finally managed to whisper.

"Very simple, Fanny. 'Yes' or 'no' is all that's necessary."

"You—you can't be serious, Stephen!"

"My darling, I was never more serious in my life. Think of the fun we can have! Honestly, Fanny, I hadn't realized what it's like to be with someone with whom I can be myself. I can't imagine going on without you. At least, I don't much want to try to do it."

"Do I really mean that much to you, Stephen?"

"More. Much, much more. Won't you consider it?"

"I don't have to consider it. Of course I'll marry you, you delightful, ridiculous man!"

For some moments neither spoke, but at last Dr. Robbertson took a deep breath and released Miss Granby.

"I'll see about the license at once. We can be married on Friday."

"Oh, Stephen!"

"We'll go away," he said. "Away from this appalling village to a place where we can be ourselves and begin to enjoy life."

"London?"

"We could, of course, but I was thinking about a little house I have near Stockholm. It's on a lovely lake. It's wonderful there in the summer."

"But in the winter?" she asked, repressing a shudder.

"In the winter we could go to the Riviera, if you wanted. Or almost any other place. Sydney, perhaps. Between us we'll have enough to do just about what we want, you know."

Miss Granby nodded, still not believing that she wasn't dreaming.

"When, Fanny?" he asked.

"Well, you said Friday. And we've really nothing to wait for, have we?"

"I rather think the waiting bit has already been overdone, my dear."

Miss Granby nodded.

"Shall we be married at St. Margaret's?" she asked.

Dr. Robbertson frowned.

"I really don't think we want so precious a memory mixed up with recollections of our saintly vicar. My London flat's in St. Bride's parish, and the rector is an old friend of my family's. Why not go up to London and make a really festive occasion of it?"

"Perfect!" exclaimed Miss Granby. "Oh!"

"What's the matter?"

"Oh, nothing really. It's just that I'll have to give notice to—to my cook."

"If I were you, Fanny, I should hang on to Boudicca if it's possible. She's a cook in a thousand. Do you think she'd like to spend her summers in Sweden?"

"You mean take her *with* us?"

"Well—scarcely *with* us. After all, honeymoons *à trois* went out in the last century. No. My idea would be to send her ahead of us to get things ready. There's an old woman there who can show her about—she speaks English fairly well—and then we'd have a comfortable place to go home to after our wedding tour."

"I'll ask her, Stephen," said Miss Granby. Then she smiled. "I really think you're marrying me for the sake of my cook!"

"How did you guess? Oh! It's nearly twelve o'clock. I must be off. Do you want to come up to London with me?"

"Dearest, there're a world of things to do here, and I'd better see Boudicca at once."

There was a long period of silence except for little sighs.

"I must go."

"Yes, dearest."

"Really, I must."

"Of course. We're still going to Wroxley, aren't we?"

"Why, yes, Fanny, if you want. We can drive back on Friday in plenty of time."

"Yes. It will be such a contrast with your last dinner there."

"I certainly hope so!" exclaimed Dr. Robbertson, laughing.

26

Lela Staine made up her mind and dialed the Hitchcock's number.

"Portia, dear. Lela."

"Oh, how *nice* to hear from you, dear. How *is* the vicar?"

"Frederick is quite well, considering that he had a—ah—rather *trying* day yesterday, thank you, dear."

"I'm *so* pleased," cooed Mrs. Hitchcock. "*Such* a shocking thing!"

"Er—have you heard how Lord Mauley is?" asked Mrs. Staine, anxious to change the subject.

"Why, no. In fact, I've not heard since yesterday. I believe that he's coming along quite nicely."

"Frederick and I thought we might walk over to the Hall. Just to inquire, you know. We—we thought that perhaps you and your husband would like to join us. Just a brief little visit, you know. Just to leave cards."

"Oh, how *thoughtful,* Lela, dear!" said Mrs. Hitchcock. Then she went on. "Is—is Lady Mauley still here?"

"Ah—yes. However, we don't expect to *stay,* you know. After all, Lady Mauley will probably be having a nap. We don't want to tire her, of course. Such a *dear* person!"

"Thomas and I will meet you at our turning, Lela. What time?"

"Rather think I shall take a little walk, Mother," said Lord Mauley as he rose from the table.

"Do," said Lady Mauley. "A little exercise would be good for you after stopping so long in bed."

Lord Mauley selected a hat and wandered off down the alley leading to the folly. The air was fresh and warm. He decided that he would walk to the folly, rest a bit, and then go round by the Carp Pond. There had been no carp in that particular sheet of water for well over a century, but it had always been called the Carp Pond. In this, as in other matters, Lord Mauley was conservative.

As he reached the intersection with the side path, he heard voices, and in a moment the Staines and the Hitchcocks were in sight. Lord Mauley waved cordially, and the visitors hastened toward him.

"Lord Mauley!" exclaimed the vicar. "What a *charming* surprise!"

"How *lovely* to see you up again!" said Mrs. Hitchcock.

"Well rested and fit, Lord Mauley," commented Mr. Hitchcock.

Lord Mauley grinned.

"Nice to be about again," he said. "Nice to see all of you. Good of you to come over, you know." He paused. "I say, I was just going to stroll over to the folly. Will you join me? Such a lovely day!"

"A *charming* idea!" exclaimed the vicar.

"A *lovely* stroll!" said Mrs. Hitchcock.

"An *extremely* lovely day!" said Mrs. Staine.

"Good!" said Mr. Hitchcock.

Lord Mauley offered an arm to each of the ladies, their spouses bringing up the rear.

"I've always *marveled* at this part of the grounds, Lord Mauley," said Mrs. Hitchcock.

"True," said Mrs. Staine. "It's pure *Brown,* isn't it? 'Calamity,' I mean," she explained.

"'Capability!'" hissed her husband from the rear.

"Umm? Of *course!* How *silly* of me!"

The Hitchcock laugh rang through what verdure there was, and an indignant rook rose, cawing in protest.

"Who designed the folly, Lord Mauley?" asked the vicar hurriedly, although he had known for years.

"My great-great-grandfather. Built it about 1780. Got the idea from something he saw in Italy."

Mr. Hitchcock muttered under his breath, "If he saw *that* thing in Italy, he was *already* mad!"

It was an unfortunately well-known fact that the Third Viscount had spent the last three decades of his existence in a strait-waistcoat.

"The *spire!*" cried Mrs. Staine. "How it *soars!* Up and up! So ethereally *uplifting!*"

"And those *marvelous* arches beneath it! Such a *richness* in those columns," said Mrs. Hitchcock. "You were very *wise* to have the gilding restored, Lord Mauley. *Such* elegance! Ah, *what* an epoch it was!"

"Lord Mauley," asked the vicar, "just where does that door lead? I've often wondered. Is there a room beyond the colonnade?"

"Oh, yes," replied Lord Mauley, surprised. "Haven't you ever been in it?"

"Why, no. I thought that perhaps it was there merely for the sake of architectural balance."

Architectural bosh! growled Mr. Hitchcock to himself. The whole bloody thing's as unbalanced as its builder!

"Oh, *do* let us see it, Lord Mauley!" exclaimed Mrs. Staine.

"Well, let me see. I think I have the key here. Umm. That's for my strongbox. *That's* the duplicate of Birkett's cellar key. Ah, here we are!"

Lord Mauley stepped forward and inserted the large brass key in the lock. After a couple of ineffectual turns in the wrong direction, the key performed its function, and the door stood open. Utter gloom was revealed.

"Ouff! It stinks!" said Lord Mauley. "Must be two years since I've been in here. There's a trick, you know, about this place, but I can't for the life of me remember what it is."

"A trick?" asked the vicar curiously.

"My ancestor was fond of all kinds of mechanical devices. Automata, you know. Birkett comes down here once a month or so with a London chap who looks after things. There's some sort of—um—practical joke—but I can't for the life of me remember *what*." He sniffed. "Awfully close, isn't it? Well, I shall have to have it aired out more often. Though the clockwork gets rusty if there's too *much* air."

"Clockwork?" asked Mrs. Staine.

"All sorts of gadgets," explained Lord Mauley. "Frankly, they bore me. The British Museum wanted to buy 'em, but, after all, one doesn't like to sell one's ancestors' belongings, does one?"

"Hmm," said Mr. Hitchcock.

"Er—may we go in?" asked Mrs. Hitchcock.

"Oh, of course. There used to be some candles. Do you see any candles, Vicar?"

"Here they are. It's quite dark, isn't it? Shall I light them?"

"Yes, you'd better, I think," said Lord Mauley, and the vicar complied.

"Now *what* is *this?*" exclaimed Mrs. Staine, looking at a huge case of carved and paneled deal picked out with gold.

Lord Mauley frowned in thought. Then he replied, "That's a machine my ancestor brought back from Germany—Saxony, as a matter of fact. There're twenty-four trumpets and two kettledrums in it.''

"What?" asked Mr. Hitchcock in disbelief.

''Yes,'' replied Lord Mauley. ''It plays marches—and things. But I can't recall how you start it.''

''What about this lever?'' asked Mr. Hitchcock, at the same time bearing down upon it.

Lord Mauley's protest was cut short by a thunderous crash as the entry door slammed of its own accord. Then there was a whir of machinery and the automaton set to work.

The room was not large, but even had it been the size of the Albert Hall, there could have been no doubt in anyone's mind that Lord Mauley had not been exaggerating. There were indubitably twenty-four trumpets, playing implacably in four-part harmony, resonantly punctuated by two most redoubtable kettledrums. That is was Handel's Grand March from *Rinaldo,* they neither knew nor cared. They simply wanted to get away from the incredible din that seemed to make the very candle flames waver in the stale air.

"Shut it off!" screamed Mrs. Hitchcock wildly. *"Shut it off!"*

"How?" bellowed the vicar, his hands over his ears.

They looked at Lord Mauley, who in turn looked stunned. He shrugged.

Mr. Hitchcock reeled to the door. It was shut fast and, apparently, locked.

The ''Grand March'' continued with its insane trills and arpeggios. For several measures the drums played alone; then the trumpets came in *sforzando,* and the vicar seriously thought he might lose his mind as well as his hearing.

After what seemed an hour, although it was actually only eight minutes, the ''Grand March'' concluded. The silence was welcome and deafening.

''That's the *trick,*'' said Lord Mauley, mopping the sweat from his forehead. ''You shouldn't've moved that lever.''

''Trick?'' asked Mr. Hitchcock wanly. Shock had dissipated any feeling of guilt.

"When you start the machine, the door automatically locks," said Lord Mauley. "I remember now."

Mrs. Hitchcock's tone was pure nitric acid.

"And *how,* my *dear* Lord Mauley, does one *open* the door again? Do you—oh, just by *chance,* of course!—*happen* to remember *that?*"

Lord Mauley's reply was inaudible as the machine struck up a spirited rendition of "See, the Conq'ring Hero Comes."

"D'ya like Handel?" yelled Mr. Hitchcock to his wife.

She shook her head and was instantly sorry. It was aching viciously.

The Staines glared at Lord Mauley like a pair of basilisks.

Lord Mauley was pottering about with various levers, but the only result was to set in motion a pastoral waxworks. Satyrs began to pursue nymphs, and shepherds raped dryads, all with the greatest eighteenth-century aplomb. When the cycle was completed, it all began over again. The spectacle was rendered still more harrowing by its movements being timed to an (inaudible) music box. The little actors were hopelessly at odds with Handel's war-horse. The result induced vertigo.

Lord Mauley's captive audience did not have to watch the puppet show, but they could not ignore the Saxon monster. At last, it came to an end with a nerve-grinding roll of drums.

There was silence.

"Is—is it going to play any more?" asked Mrs. Hitchcock faintly.

"I—I think there're a couple of hymn tunes—and—and I rather think it plays 'Rule, Britannia,' too," said Lord Mauley hesitantly, for he was aware, he thought, of a sudden drop in the temperature of the social atmosphere.

"My God!" murmured the vicar, lifting his eyes.

The machine not only played Lord Mauley's recollected program, but it went on to "The King of Prushia's March," "Thus Speeds Away Each Cherish'd Hour," "Belov'd, Thy Tears These Sods Bedew," and concluded with a rousing performance of "God Save the King"—twelve variations—with embellishments.

Lord Mauley now definitely sensed a certain impatience in his guests.

Mrs. Hitchcock laughed hysterically, and her husband groaned.

The vicar clenched his fists, and his wife sobbed.

Lord Mauley wiped his forehead again and tried the door. It was still locked.

27

The candles were guttering and the air was becoming uncomfortably heavy.

The vicar was still suffering from the events of the previous day, and his always-superficial self-control was not equal to the situation.

"Do you mean, sir," he rasped, "that the only way we can leave this—this hellhole—is by hearing that damnable contraption again?"

Reluctantly Lord Mauley nodded.

"*All* of it?" whimpered Mrs. Staine.

"Damnation!" exclaimed the vicar. "Mauley, you're a doddering psychopathic ass!"

"Frederick!"

"Oh, *shut up,* Lela!" The vicar glowered at Lord Mauley. "This is just what I might have expected of you! It's of a piece with your allowing that *male whore* to drive all over your grounds! It's just like you!"

"I'm frightfully sorry, you know," said Lord Mauley, to whom the vicar's remarks made no sense whatever.

"Sorry!" exclaimed Mr. Hitchcock, giving the vicar an eloquent glance.

"You *imbecile!*" shouted the vicar, approaching his cowering and bewildered host. "You bloody, dithering, incompetent, fucked-up *fool!*"

Mrs. Hitchcock, for once, was speechless.

Mrs. Staine swallowed and took a deep breath.

"Let's—let's get it over with—and get out," she said hoarsely.

They watched dismally as the shaken Lord Mauley inserted a crank and wound up the mechanism. No one looked at the vicar.

They shuddered as Lord Mauley pressed the starting lever.

"Where in the world can Charlie be?" asked Mrs. Tunstall, buttering a muffin. "It's getting close to dark."

"He's probably gone into the village," said Lady Mauley. "Perhaps to the Rose. He's not been about much lately, you know."

"There it is again!" exclaimed Miss Pollock.

"There's what again, Agnes?" asked Mrs. Tunstall.

"Listen. Don't you hear music? I thought I heard it earlier, but I wasn't sure."

Faintly, borne on the breeze, came the plaintive strains of "Belov'd, Thy Tears These Sods Bedew."

"Someone's wireless, I suppose," said Lady Mauley, pouring herself another cup of tea.

"Yes, or a gramophone," said Mr. Tunstall.

Mrs. Tunstall was frowning.

"No—it sounds—" Her face cleared. "I know what it is! The Deaf-Mute's Delight!"

"What?" asked Miss Pollock, puzzled.

"It's that machine in the folly. You remember, Agnes. The drum-and-trumpet monstrosity."

"'Musick that goeth with a Wheele,'" said Mr. Tunstall reminiscently.

"Charlie is probably down there playing it. I hope it doesn't cause a relapse! I'm not likely to forget that tune. Do you remember, Philip, when we were trapped in the place?"

"I wish I could forget it, Jean. I've always thought you deliberately planned that little tête-à-tête."

Mrs. Tunstall laughed. (Her husband had finally come to

the point and proposed during their three-hour incarceration.)

"I didn't really, Philip, but once we were there, I found it convenient to forget the other door the machine conceals. It was the threat of hearing it again that decided you, wasn't it?"

"My dear Jean, I would have proposed to Lela Staine to avoid hearing it a second time!"

"Perhaps," said Lady Mauley, "I should ask the Staines over for tea—I've rather neglected them this time—and then take them down to the folly."

"Lady Mauley, I'd not wish that on even the Staines!"

"Or even the Hitchcocks?" asked Mrs. Tunstall.

"Or even the Hitchcocks," replied her husband.

"Well," said Lady Mauley, "I must have my nap before dinner."

They rose as she got out of her chair.

"How do you feel, Agnes?" she asked.

"Much better than I have any right to feel, Cousin Emily. While you're resting, I think I shall write some letters. I may walk into the village to post them. I should rather like a bit of exercise, and it's still fairly light."

"Do as you like, Agnes. I shall see you and Jean presently," said Lady Mauley, nodding to her son-in-law and his wife. She left with Miss Pollock.

"Give me another cup of tea, please, Jean."

"Very well. I'd like to congratulate you, my dear. You were quite sweet to Charlie at lunch. I appreciated it."

"Oh, well."

"Philip, you look as if you'd swallowed a canary and are now contemplating the birdseed. What do you know that you're not telling me?"

Her husband, delighted with the opportunity, told her.

Mrs. Tunstall raised her eyes to the Thornhill ceiling.

"Really! What can you do with Mother!"

"You can't do anything with her, Jean. No one can. That's one of the reasons I'm so very fond of her."

"But—if you're not just making a good story of this—what must the servants have thought?" She paused. "Do you suppose Mother *really* understands? I mean, well, from what you tell me about those two young men—"

"Oh, Jean! Don't be naive, my dear!"

"Of course, there *was* Uncle Lawrence—"

"Exactly. You don't think your mother really believed her brother had to live permanently on the Continent because he had a tendency to gout, do you?" Mr. Tunstall laughed. "Do you remember Alistair's parody of that Victorian quatrain, 'We never mention Aunt Clara'?"

"Not all of it," she said, shaking her head. "How did Alistair's go?"

Her husband placed one hand upon his chest, lifted the other toward the ceiling, and declaimed.

"We never discuss Uncle Lawrence!
Though 'tis twenty-five years since he fled,
he *still* lives with that wrestler in Florence.
Father says they'd be better off dead."

Mrs. Tunstall smiled.

"He was delightful, wasn't he? I'm sorry he's dead."

"Yes, and his lover, too. A long and faithful relationship."

"But then, Julia Dodridge—and Thelma Mullen! Philip, can you picture them in such a milieu?"

"Jean, where your mother is concerned, I can picture anything—once it occurs to me! Anyhow, although Julia can be a little starchy at times, Thelma certainly isn't stuffy."

She laughed quietly.

"I dare say you're going to be devilish, Philip?"

"What do you mean?"

"You're going to tell Neddy Wroxshire?"

Mr. Tunstall grinned. Then he shook his head in mock regret.

"I should dearly like to, but—well, it was really a bit

much, Jean. It doesn't place your mother in a very gracious light."

Mrs. Tunstall sighed.

"No, it certainly doesn't," she said ruefully. Then, in spite of herself, she laughed.

"I should have loved to see the bishop roaring about the park! Oh, what a pity we didn't come a day earlier!"

"Yes," said her husband, "I'd thought of that, too, and—why here's Charlie!"

Lord Mauley entered the drawing room. He was gray-faced, and his stomach sagged even more than his shoulders. He tottered toward the tea table and flopped into a chair.

"Charlie!" exclaimed his sister. "What's the matter? Aren't you feeling well?"

Lord Mauley turned tortured eyes upon the pair, eyes that had gazed into the depths of human depravity.

"I should like some tea, Jean," was all he said, but he said it in the manner of a condemned man requesting to see the chaplain once more.

"Of course, dear."

"What's wrong, Charlie?" asked his brother-in-law.

Lord Mauley closed tortured eyes and shook his head.

"Nothing," he said.

"Did you walk into the village?" asked Mrs. Tunstall.

"No."

"Were you at the folly?" asked Mr. Tunstall. "We were sure we heard the Deaf-Mute's Delight."

Lord Mauley flinched, but he said nothing and held out a shaking hand for his teacup.

Mr. Tunstall exchanged glances with his wife and said nothing further.

Mrs. Tunstall continued to watch her brother, puzzled. His had never been a particularly commanding presence, but now he exuded total despondency.

"Charlie, dear, you've tried to do too much on your first day up. You look tired. Why don't you go upstairs? I'll tell Birkett to send you up a nice supper tray. I've brought some books for you; one of them's that new French book on porcelain. You can relax and have a quiet evening."

Lord Mauley tried to smile, but the effort was not a success. He decided that uncomplaining fortitude was preferable.

"I—I suppose I *am* rather tired. I—I hadn't thought of that. I think I *shall* go to bed, Jean. Will you ask Birkett to have them send up something, then? Some pale sherry, I think—and some lobster mayonnaise—and—and, yes, one of those meringues with marzipan."

"Of course, Charlie. I'll remember."

Lord Mauley set down his untasted tea and went slowly from the room, one hand upon his chest, tortured eyes upon the carpet. It was tolerably effective, but Mrs. Siddons would no doubt have done it differently.

"Well! What do you make of *that,* Jean?"

"I don't know what to think, Philip. Something has evidently seriously upset him."

"I dare say he's just tired. After all, if he's been listening to that thing in the folly, it's not surprising."

"Possibly you're right, though I've never seen him like this." She thought for a moment. "He looks martyred," she added.

His brother-in-law, as a martyr to anything but the consequences of gluttony was a new idea to Philip Tunstall.

"He'll be all right in the morning," he said uneasily.

28

The vicar and his wife sat before the study fire, outwardly placid. The evening had turned cool, and the vicarage was damp. In the light of the flames and of the lamps, Mrs. Staine worked doggedly at her needlepoint. Her husband was ostensibly reading *The Daughter of Time.* Occasionally, Mrs. Staine glanced across at him, wondering if he was really reading. As the minutes passed and the vicar did not turn a single page, Mrs. Staine's suspicion became a certainty. She wondered whether she should break in upon her husband's withdrawn mood. They had spoken scarcely two words to one another (or to anyone else) since leaving the folly.

Mrs. Staine was rather out of practice in making apologies, but she swallowed and spoke.

"I'm sorry, Frederick."

"Umm?"

"Oh, Frederick, don't try to pretend that you're reading! You haven't turned a page for over forty minutes."

The vicar closed the book and stared at his wife.

"*You're* sorry?" he asked in a puzzled fashion. "For going there, you mean? No. It—it was my fault. I was very wrong to say the things I said—to you—to everyone."

"It was a very trying afternoon," said his wife comfortingly.

"Yes—yes, it was. Most regrettable."

"Lord Mauley—" began Mrs. Staine. Her husband interrupted her.

"My dear Lela, I shall be frank. I am henceforth utterly indifferent to Charles Mauley."

"Oh, Frederick."

"I mean it, Lela. We've always known that he is not precisely at the—ah—apex of human intellect, but I had thought heretofore that he was rather more sensible than events have proved."

"But it wasn't really his fault, Frederick. Thomas Hitchcock should never have tampered with that wretched machine."

"It's Mauley's property, isn't it? Wouldn't you think that any reasonably sane creature could have remembered what would happen? Couldn't remember the trick, indeed! Why didn't he warn us before he ever took us into the place?"

"But—but *is* he reasonably sane?" asked Mrs. Staine, almost trembling at her audacity.

"No," said the vicar.

"Things are going to be rather awkward, you know, Frederick."

"What do you suppose I've been thinking about for the last three hours?" growled the vicar. "And after all my attentions to him, too," he added in a hurt tone.

"Yes, dear, I know," said Mrs. Staine soothingly.

"I—I shall send my resignation to that cretin at the Hall, and then I shall write to the bishop."

"The *bishop?*" Mrs. Staine sounded fearful.

"Yes. I shall ask Bishop Dodridge if he can't contrive to arrange something for me."

"But—after yesterday?"

"Oh, nonsense, my dear! I smoothed *that* over very nicely," said the vicar, with a faint touch of returning complacency. It was not up to his usual standard, but it encouraged his wife.

"Perhaps," she said slowly, "the bishop *could* arrange something for you." She thought. "Do you think the duke could help you?"

"What duke?" asked the vicar absently. His mind had wandered back to the first Vespa incident.

Mrs. Staine was surprised.

"Why, the Duke of Wroxshire, Frederick."

"That *Dodridge* woman's brother?" he asked incredulously.

"Well, it's true that she's not very cordial, but still—" That Mrs. Dodridge might gladly expedite their departure, was, perhaps, Mrs. Staine's unconscious thought. If so, however, by the time the idea had surfaced to the conscious level, she expressed it differently. "After all, Frederick, Mrs. Dodridge and the bishop are very fond of each other. If she could oblige him by helping one of his clergy, I'm sure you'd find her very willing to help you."

"Oh, no, Lela."

"Let's think about it, dear."

"Well . . ."

Thomas Hitchcock chuckled.

"I can see nothing to be so cheerful about," said his wife impatiently.

"Can't you, Portia? No. Probably not."

"Well?"

There was a long pause, and Mrs. Hitchcock became even more impatient.

"*Well,* Thomas?"

"Simply, my dear Portia, that in a day or two I shall call upon Lord Mauley and tender my most heartfelt apologies."

"What!"

"Why not? What have I to lose? Or you? Whereas if we indulge ourselves in a state of righteous indignation, we are going to find living in Cherton rather a sticky proposition. No, Portia. Lord Mauley is not worth the embarrassment and the social tension that a rift would create in so small a place as this. Would you want to leave your house and your gardens just because that fool at the Hall *is* a fool? *Remember!* He can terminate our lease at will!"

"But surely he wouldn't ask us to leave? Not after all the money we've spent on this place!"

"Of course not. But I'm being practical. Besides"—he leered at his wife—"how would you like Cherton *sans* Staines?"

"Without the Staines?"

"Yes. Staineless."

"What *do* you mean, Thomas?"

"My dear Portia! Didn't you notice how I kept urging the vicar to greater efforts, once I saw how he'd lost control of himself? Didn't you notice how, while ostensibly trying to compose matters, I did everything I could to persuade Staine to make an even greater ass of himself? *Especially* when we got outside and he began to flag! *That* was when he surpassed his previous triumphs!" Mr. Hitchcock smirked. "Oh, it was *clever* of me, my dear! It was, if I may say so, *pure* statesmanship!"

Mrs. Hitchcock was impressed.

"Oh, Thomas! How *crafty* of you!"

Mr. Hitchcock rubbed his hands and chuckled again.

"I dare say Staine and that precious wife of his are in a cold sweat at this very moment."

"Do you think that—that the vicar will have second thoughts? Do you think he'll apologize, too?"

"Don't be ridiculous, Portia! How could he? After what *he* said? My dear, I wouldn't've spelled some of his expressions, let alone given voice to them! Why, he was still screaming at poor Mauley when you and I fled. What vituperation! It was almost as good as one of Luther's earthier remonstrances to the pope." Again Mr. Hitchcock chuckled.

Mrs. Hitchcock felt decidedly better. She even managed a smile.

"Portia, let's have an old-fashioned posset. Lots of wine and spices. Use the silver bowls, what? I'll light the fire while you're getting things ready. We'll have a cheerful evening after all!"

"Oh, Thomas, you *are* so adroit!" she purred.

"Yes," said her husband, adjusting his tie, "I rather fancy I *am*."

"Your uncle's spending a lot of time with Miss Granby these days," said Dirk as he rose from his armchair to turn off the television set.

"Yeh," said Tommy, looking at his friend. "How's ya head?"

"I think it's going to stay on my neck, Tommy. My God! What a party! You feel all right, kid?"

"Yeh. Jus' horny, sweetie," said Tommy, removing his bikini.

Dirk grinned.

"What else's new?" he asked, sitting on the arm of Tommy's chair.

Tommy ran one hand through Dirk's black locks and winked at him.

"We gonna go to London like ya said?"

"Sure. Anytime."

"I got a idea, Dirk."

Dirk rose to pick Tommy up in his arms.

"I've got one, too. I'll take you upstairs, and you can tell me about it. *Damn,* but you're a beauty!"

29

Lord Mauley was tempted to have his breakfast in bed, pleading fatigue. He was still shaken, and the thought of facing his mother at the breakfast table was not conducive to tranquility. Lord Mauley meditated. He decidedly wished to drive up to London. There was a sale of the late Dowager Lady Porford's effects, and he had long had an eye upon a Sèvres statuette of Madame de Pompadour's dog. Lord Mauley had, at considerable expense, acquired a statuette of the marquise as Galatea; he felt it only decent to reunite the lady and her dog, since the only possible figurine of Louis XV was in a famous London collection. He considered the matter as he shaved and as Birkett helped him to dress and as he walked down the stairs.

Lady Mauley was already at her place, radiating a cheer that, in view of the hour, her son found not only depressing but indecent.

"Good morning, Charlie. You look *much* better this morning. Jean tells me you were rather knocked up last night and went to bed early. Evidently your night's rest has done you good."

"Ah, yes, Mother."

"Have some sausages. They're excellent. I had Cartwright's mother send them over from Wroxley yesterday."

"Umm—yes. Very nice."

Lord Mauley looked at the sausages and asked for a cup of coffee.

"I shall drive up to London this morning," he said. "There's a sale—Freddie Porford's mother's collection of china."

"An admirable idea," said Lady Mauley, nodding approval. "You do need to get about a bit. Perhaps you can find something pretty there. Mary Porford had some lovely things."

"Umm, yes," said Lord Mauley. Then he asked, "The bishop—Bishop Dodridge—is he still in Cherton?"

"He was to be here until tomorrow."

"Ah," said Lord Mauley, rising from his untasted breakfast.

"Aren't you going to eat anything?" demanded his mother.

"I—I'm not particularly hungry. I had some biscuits with my early tea."

"Umgh!" said Lady Mauley.

"Bishop, this is Charlie Mauley."

"Good morning, Lord Mauley. I'm glad to hear you're recovering. I hope that you've not had any serious problems as a result of your illness?"

Lord Mauley said what he thought was necessary. The bishop listened patiently.

"Ah," continued Lord Mauley, "I—I—ah, wondered if you could possibly drop by for tea this afternoon? There's something—a matter I should like to discuss with you. It's rather—it's rather a delicate—um—matter."

"Why, yes, Lord Mauley. I should be very glad to see you."

"Good, Bishop. About four?"

It was not until he had rung off that Lord Mauley realized that he might not have time to do justice to Lady Porford's sale and return to Cherton by four. He shrugged. He would have to manage it, he decided.

Lady Mauley looked at her daughter.

''You know, Jean,'' she said, ''I've been rather naughty.''

''Do you mean that you've murdered someone, Mother?''

''Well, no. But I've been rather offhand with the Staines.'' She thought. ''Do you think that you and Philip could possibly bear to have the Staines here for tea this afternoon?''

''Oh, *Mother!*''

''My dear, I feel precisely the same way, but this *is* Charlie's house, you know, and I ought to try to keep things reasonably comfortable for him. The vicar was most—ah, attentive during Charlie's illness.''

''Oh, very well, Mother. I'll tell Philip. He'll be *so* pleased.''

''And you *accepted?*'' asked Mrs. Staine in astonishment.

''Yes. Mauley is in London for the day. He's gone to a sale. You know what the ass is like when he sees a bit of china.''

''Really, Frederick, you should try to moderate your expressions.''

''You know my position, Lela. I shall adhere to it.''

''Oh, very well. About four, I think you said?''

''Yes, Lela. About four.''

Mrs. Staine clasped her hands in her lap and sighed.

''When are you going to talk to the bishop?'' she asked.

''I have decided to write to the bishop. This sort of thing is best initiated through formal correspondence.''

''He's still here, you know.''

''That may be. However, unless he sees fit to call upon me here, I am not likely to encounter him. I prefer to conduct the matter in my *own* way, Lela.''

''Very well, Frederick.''

''I know that your advice and suggestions are well meant, but I think that in this matter I must be guided by my sense of fitness—and, ah, discretion.''

''Yes, Frederick.''

"You agree?"

"Yes, Frederick."

"You consider my position—reasonable?"

"Yes—Frederick."

"Lady Mauley is a woman of some importance. I should not wish to antagonize her. It is very kind of her to ask us. Plainly, she is not a party to her son's abominable stupidity, and I think that we should be remiss in refusing her invitation. It would be—ah—impolitic."

"But how *dreadful* it would be were Lord Mauley to return while we're there!"

"Lady Mauley assured me that he will be gone for the day."

"She *said* as much?" asked Mrs. Staine.

"She said that Mauley had gone to Lady Porford's sale. We may take it as a certainty that he'll not be back until very late. If he *should* come—mind you, I'm sure that he *won't*—we shall simply excuse ourselves in a dignified manner, acting with true Christian fortitude. Perhaps you had best feign a slight headache. It can get worse if Mauley comes back."

Mrs. Staine tightened her hands and refrained from observing that the headache she had had for eighteen hours was already more than sufficient.

30

Lord Mauley returned to the Hall in a mood of self-congratulatory complacence. Not only had he acquired the coveted dog but his agent had succeeded in outbidding rivals when, to Lord Mauley's astonishment, there appeared a duplicate of the Louis XV he had so often eyed in Manchester Square. The two precious figures, carefully packed, rested upon the seat beside him, and Lord Mauley plagued Cartwright all the way back with exhortations of caution. By the time the youth turned in at the Hall gates, he was almost frantic to begin his job with Lady Mauley.

Lord Mauley recalled that the bishop was to come at four; it was scarcely that yet. Upon reaching the Hall, he hastened to his bedroom to change.

"Where's my mother, Birkett?"

"In the drawing room, sir. Her ladyship and Mrs. Tunstall are expecting—"

"Oh," said Lord Mauley, interrupting Birkett, "Mother knows, does she? Then I shan't have to hurry quite so much. I was afraid he might already be here."

"No, sir," said Birkett, only partly comprehending his employer. He made no further effort. It was so useless, he thought.

"Good," said Lord Mauley.

"Where can they have got to?" asked Mrs. Tunstall, looking at the clock. "It's well past four."

"The vicar is usually quite punctual," said Lady Mauley. "I do wish they'd arrive. The sooner begun, the sooner ended."

Philip Tunstall said nothing but he thought unprintable thoughts. As fond as he was of his mother-in-law, Lady Mauley's decision to afflict him with the Staines made him wonder whether tea wasn't considerably thicker than blood.

"I think someone is coming now," he sighed mournfully.

Whittaker announced Bishop Dodridge.

"Why, Bishop!" exclaimed Lady Mauley. "What a delightful surprise! How good of you to call!"

The bishop replied in kind, wondering at the almost effusive greeting he received from the ordinarily taciturn Philip Tunstall.

"My son has just returned from London, Bishop. He'll be down in a moment."

"Well, it's nice to see you again, Bishop," said Mrs. Tunstall. She meditated for a split second and then happily plunged on. "The Staines are coming in, too. Quite a pleasant afternoon, isn't it?"

The bishop said nothing, smiling like patience on a monument.

"Where's Julia?" asked Lady Mauley. "Why didn't you bring her?"

"Why, I suppose I should explain—"

The bishop stopped explaining as Lord Mauley entered.

After the necessary civilities had been gotten through, Lord Mauley looked at his mother, wondering whether she had ordered tea. Lady Mauley seemed in no hurry, so her son turned rather nervously to the bishop.

"Ah, Bishop—I—ah—I've just acquired a pair of rather charming Sèvres figures. Perhaps you'd care to see them before we have tea."

The bishop understood that this was a ploy to get him out of the drawing room.

"Why, I should like to very much, Lord Mauley. My wife will be interested to hear about them. She's really quite envious of the fine collection you're accumulating."

"Run along, Charlie," said Lady Mauley. "We'll see them later. Don't be too long, though. The—"

But Lord Mauley was through the door and out of hearing. The bishop followed less precipitately.

"I see," said the bishop gravely. "You know, Lord Mauley, while it might be possible to arrange another living for Mr. Staine, it would be necessary to have his consent. He would have to resign this one voluntarily, and at present I don't know of anything that would be likely to tempt him. St. Margaret's is one of the best in the diocese, you know."

Lord Mauley's mouth opened and shut like that of a landed fish. The bishop went on hurriedly.

"However, I can quite understand your position in view of the really appalling things you've told me. I—I have not been entirely satisfied, if I may say so in confidence, with Mr. Staine. From what you tell me of his behavior of yesterday, I am considerably less than satisfied. The matter will have to be carefully investigated. Mr. Staine may be ill. At any rate, Lord Mauley, I shall try to arrange things with as little embarrassment and annoyance as possible, but you will understand that my authority is limited.''

Lord Mauley nodded.

''At the same time,'' the bishop continued, ''I must say that, considering what you tell me, I *am* astonished that the vicar and Mrs. Staine should be coming here to tea this afternoon.''

Lord Mauley gave a salmonlike leap, his eyes glassy.

"Here?" he asked faintly. ''The vicar's coming *here*?''

''You didn't know, then?'' asked the bishop.

''I've only just come down from London. My—my mother must've asked them.''

''Oh, dear,'' said the bishop, frowning, ''that *is* rather awkward, isn't it?''

''Awkward!'' exclaimed Lord Mauley. ''It's—it's outrageous!''

''Lady Mauley knows about this—contretemps—with the vicar?''

''No,'' said Lord Mauley slowly, ''I don't suppose she does. I—I didn't say anything to anyone about it.''

''Most unfortunate,'' said the bishop. Then he went on. ''Lord Mauley, why don't you allow me to tell Lady Mauley that your trip has tired—"

Lady Mauley appeared at the door.

''Charlie! You and the bishop must come into the drawing room. We're all waiting for you.''

''Grrgkh!''

''What's that Charlie?'' Lady Mauley tapped her stick impatiently. ''Do come, Charlie! Bishop, bring him in. I'm afraid the tea's going to get cold.''

The atmosphere of the drawing room, the bishop thought as they went in, was enough to turn the tea into ice.

''Good afternoon, Bishop,'' said Mrs. Staine desperately.

''A pleasant meeting,'' said her husband, looking anywhere

but at Lord Mauley, who had sat down without so much as a nod to the Staines.

The bishop wondered, not for the first time, what diabolical influence had possessed him to visit Cherton. He began talking at random. He discussed the weather, past, present, and future, with a thoroughness that made the Tunstalls wonder whether he had taken leave of his senses. Lady Mauley said what she could, glowering at her son, who, disconcertingly, glowered back. Philip Tunstall, usually considering himself above such meteorological chitchat, felt the tension and joined in, not daring to look at his wife.

"Of course," the bishop babbled, "at this time of year, the weather *is* so changeable. I've seldom seen such a spring, though. One wonders if winter has really left us for good or if it's really still with us, you know. Of course, it will make up for it in the summer, no doubt, but still it is rather disheartening for the moment."

"It's not really seasonable, is it?" said Mr. Tunstall, hoping he wasn't blushing. "Perhaps it all has something to do with sunspots?"

Mrs. Tunstall could not understand her husband's brightly idiotic manner, but she understood a good deal and joined the weather report.

"Such a dreadful lot of mud, too," she said. "It makes motoring quite hazardous. The roads are so slippery that there're sure to be accidents. I dare say even cyclists have problems, don't you?"

The vicar went white, the bishop a lovely episcopal violet.

"Well, Bishop," said Philip Tunstall, kicking his wife under cover of the tea table, "I suppose summer really *will* arrive one day."

"It usually *does*," remarked Lady Mauley acidly. "Where's Agnes?"

Mr. Tunstall was thankful for a change of subject.

"She's gone into the village," he said. "She had some shopping to do."

"Ah, *how* is Miss Pollock?" asked the bishop with a solicitude implying that he hadn't seen her for years.

"Just the same," said Lady Mauley resignedly, wondering whether if they'd all gone mad.

Mrs. Staine suddenly stood up.

"Lady Mauley," she said in a trembling voice, "I—I—know you'll forgive me. I—I have the most *ghastly* headache. I thought the walk over here would do it good, but I'm afraid it hasn't. Would you think me *frightfully* rude if we left you?"

Lady Mauley expressed instant commiseration and assured Mrs. Staine that bed was the best place for such an affliction. When she was quite certain that the vicar was also leaving, she ventured an offer of brandy and lavender-salts. The Staines were polite but firm in their refusal of such delights; they left *en cortège,* the vicar solicitously supporting his anguished spouse. Lord Mauley remaining seated and, apparently, oblivious.

"Well!" exclaimed Mrs. Tunstall as the door shut.

Except for a feeling of gratitude, the bishop's mind was a blank.

"What *is* the matter with you, Charlie?" asked Lady Mauley irritably. "You look like a stricken sheep."

31

Mrs. Dodridge glanced up from her book as her brother-in-law came into the room.

"How did you find them all?" she asked.

The bishop said nothing for a moment. Then he cleared his throat.

"May I have a whiskey and soda, please, Julia?"

"So that's how you found them," she said, rising to ring.

The bishop sat down, frowning.

"Julia, why do you suppose a man goes into the Church?"

"What?"

"When I was a young man," said the bishop wearily, "I thought that I might be best able to help others if I took orders." He shook his head. "What a world!"

"Good heavens! My poor Charles, what is the matter? I've never seen you so despondent!"

The bishop rallied slightly and smiled ruefully.

"I try not to show it, even to Margaret, but—sometimes . . ." He frowned again and then looked at his sister-in-law. "Julia—tell me. Has Cherton always been like this?"

"Oh, dear! I'm afraid your little holiday hasn't been of much use to you. I'd so hoped you could relax and forget your problems for a while."

"My dear Julia, I feel that another such little holiday would be the death of me. Thank God—I say it in all reverence—thank God I'm leaving tomorrow!"

"Charles! You *are* upset! Won't you tell me what is wrong?"

The bishop sighed.

"I should like to, Julia, but I'm afraid I can't. It's a confidential matter. Obviously, of course, you can guess that it has to do with Cherton."

"I could guess that it has something to do with the vicar."

The bishop said nothing further, but his face spoke volumes.

Edwards entered with the tray. After her departure, the bishop raised his eyebrows.

"Is Edwards telepathic?" he asked.

"No," said Mrs. Dodridge. "Alcoholic refreshment seemed in order after a visit to the Hall."

"You're most understanding, Julia."

"I try to be, Charles. Heaven knows I get enough practice."

"But, you—you fool," growled Lady Mauley to her son, "why didn't you *tell* me? It would have been the easiest thing in the world to tell those wretched Staines that I had a headache or that Agnes was in labor!"

"I—I suppose I was—" Lord Mauley's voice dropped, "was—too—hurt."

Lady Mauley felt that she had been unduly severe.

"Umgh! Perhaps I ought not to've spoken so sharply, Charlie. I beg your pardon, my dear. I suppose I'm upset, too. A ghastly afternoon for everyone!"

"Yes, Mother."

"Well, there's no use crying over spilled milk," said Lady Mauley. "If you can get rid of that fool of a vicar, *tant mieux*."

"Yes, Mother."

"Hah!" exclaimed Lady Mauley.

"What is it, Mother?"

"An idea's just occurred to me. Do you remember Sydney Markby?"

"Sydney Markby?" said Lord Mauley vaguely. "Old Bolton's youngest son?"

Lady Mauley nodded.

"Sydney Markby has a parish about twelve miles from Maulcaster. I think he's done quite well there, but I'm sure he'd like a change. His wife doesn't like that part of England very much."

"But—you mean—get Staine to go *there* and have Syd come *here*, Mother?"

"Precisely," said Lady Mauley, mildly astonished by her son's rapid comprehension.

"I always liked Syd," said Lord Mauley.

"He's not the vicar of *my* parish, of course," said Lady Mauley hastily.

"Oh, Frederick, how *dreadful* it all was!"

"It was unfortunate, of course, but I don't think—the embarrassment aside—that any harm has been done. It was just as well that the bishop was present."

"It would've been *ghastly* if he hadn't."

"Hadn't what, Lela?"

"Hadn't been there."

"There? Oh—yes. There."

"When are you going to write to the bishop?"

"I have changed my plan, Lela," said the vicar, suddenly getting up.

"Frederick! What *do* you *mean*?"

"I mean that the affair has gone on long enough. I cannot bear this suspense. I shall call upon the bishop tonight."

"At Mrs. *Dodridge*'s?"

"At Mrs. Dodridge's, yes."

And the vicar went into the passage to the telephone.

"It's for you, my lord," said Edwards.

The bishop went to the telephone and unsuspectingly spoke into the mouthpiece. Then he winced. Mrs. Dodridge, in the drawing room, could not see the bishop's face but she could hear his voice, and she listened shamelessly.

"Ah—yes, Vicar."

"You mean now, Vicar?"

"I see. Why, yes. Of course."

"I *quite* understand. Well, shall we say at about half-past nine, Vicar?"

"Very well. Good-bye, Vicar."

Mrs. Dodridge was busily making a highball when her brother-in-law returned.

"I suppose you heard *that*," he said gloomily.

"Why, yes, Charles. I must say that I did. He's coming here?"

"I'm afraid so. It seems . . ." he paused as the telephone rang again.

"We're very popular tonight," said Mrs. Dodridge. "Yes, Edwards?"

"It's for the bishop, ma'am. Lady Mauley."

The bishop and Mrs. Dodridge exchanged glances, and the bishop rose. Mrs. Dodridge felt she could bear no more and quietly shut the door. Then she returned to the drinks tray and splashed more Scotch into her glass.

"Bishop? Emily Mauley here."

"Oh, Lady Mauley! Thank you for a most pleasant afternoon."

"Bishop, it scarcely becomes a member of the episcopal bench to treat the truth so carelessly!"

"I beg your pardon, Lady Mauley?"

"You know as well as I that this afternoon was utterly and preternaturally grim. It was your presence alone that forestalled battle, murder, and sudden death."

In spite of himself, he grinned.

"So Lord Mauley has told you?" he asked.

"He has," said Lady Mauley. "The situation is impossible. Can you do anything about it, Bishop?"

"Well, I've scarcely had time, you know, Lady Mauley. I shall certainly do whatever I *can* do when I return to my office tomorrow."

"Splendid! I was sure you would. Now! . . . I happen to know a man who would be suitable in every way for St. Margaret's."

The bishop raised his eyes to the ceiling.

"Yes, Lady Mauley?" he asked resignedly.

"Sydney Markby. He's at St. Swithin's at Pelham Abbas. Willie Grossmith is his bishop. The living is in the bishop's gift, you know."

"I know Bishop Grossmith fairly well," said Bishop Dodridge cautiously. "Does—does Mr. Markby want to leave St. Swithin's?"

"Probably as much as Mr. Staine wants to leave St. Margaret's—although for rather different reasons," said Lady Mauley.

"I see. Well, of course, I can promise nothing, you know, but I assure you that I shall do what I can. Yes. Yes. Good night, Lady Mauley."

Mrs. Dodridge was struck by the resignation of the bishop's expression.

"Here, Charles," she said.

He took the highball.

"Have I time for another after this one?" he asked wistfully.

"Yes," said his sister-in-law nastily. "I've told Edwards to put dinner back—just in case the Archbishop or the Queen should telephone."

"Thank you, Julia," said the bishop, grateful for her levity. He sipped his drink with becoming meekness and tried to think of nothing.

32

The following morning, Miss Granby was about to tackle Boudicca when she realized that perhaps it would be well to break the news first to at least one of her acquaintances. Once Boudicca spoke to her family about the impending move, it would be all over the village. Mr. Hoare was discreet enough, but his wife possessed the happy combination of ears and mouth equally and impartially open.

Mulling over the problem—and her acquaintances—Miss Granby at length decided upon Portia Hitchcock. Lela Staine could never get anything straight, and Miss Granby felt that she did not know either Mrs. Dodridge or Lady Thelma well enough for such a shattering confidence.

Having made sure that the kitchen door was shut, Miss Granby dialed the Hitchcocks' number. A monotone growl announced that Thomas Hitchcock was there. As Miss Granby waited for his wife, she tried to frame her announcement.

"*Good* morning, my dear Fanny! How are you this lovely, *lovely* spring day?"

Miss Granby replied that she was quite well; then she went on. "I have some news, Portia. I wanted to let you know." She paused as some electrical interference chattered on the wire.

"What's that, Fanny? What did you say? News, you said? There's something wrong with this connection, I think."

"Yes," said Miss Granby, raising her voice discreetly. "I'm going to be married to Stephen Robbertson." (There! She'd said it!)

For a moment there was silence. Whether it was stunned or not, Miss Granby was unable to decide. Then there came the premonitory arpeggio of the Hitchcock laugh.

"Really, this connection is *abominable,* Fanny! It's so *utterly* laughable—but, do you know—it sounds so *silly*—but it sounded *exactly* as if you said you were going to marry Dr. Robbertson!"

And the laugh in all its glory knifed its way through Miss Granby's head.

When she could command her temper and her hearing, Miss Granby cleared her throat and spoke. "That's *exactly* what I said, Portia!"

"Umm—yes, dear. But what was it you *did* say? So amusing a misunderstanding, *n'est-ce pas?* . . . Hello? Hello? Are you there, Fanny?"

Miss Granby was not there. She was stalking to the kitchen, striking her palms together and swearing viciously under her breath. For a moment, she paused before the door. Then she squared her shoulders and opened it.

"No!" exclaimed Mrs. Staine in disbelief.

"Yes!" screamed Mrs. Hitchcock in ecstasy.

"She *told* you that? She *really* did?"

"Not *five* minutes ago, my dear Lela."

"You—you *don't* think that *perhaps*—she—she'd been—um, *drinking?*"

"At *nine* in the *morning?*" asked Mrs. Hitchcock, struck by the idea.

"Well, you know, people who—ah, *indulge*—don't really care *what* hour of the day they—"

"Oh, nonsense, Lela! You know as well as I do that while Fanny may be slightly mad, she's not a dipsomaniac. No, she said *quite* clearly—though I really couldn't believe it—that she's going to marry Stephen Robbertson."

"How *extraordinary!*"

"That's what *I* thought."

"Will they live at his house or at hers?" asked Mrs. Staine.

"Fanny didn't say. But I dare say you'll be hearing from her. Well, I *must* ring off. I suppose I should congratulate the doctor?" And, laughing at the prospect, Mrs. Hitchcock rang off.

Tommy paused in his attempt to serve a tennis ball and waved at the large black car passing in the road. The bishop cheerfully waved back and pressed harder upon the accelerator.

Dirk stood at the other end of the court, grinning at Tommy's struggles with his racquet, for neither Tommy nor he knew anything about tennis, in spite of the doctor's attempts to teach them. Their chief reason for using the court was to improve their tans, and for this purpose, they wore swimming suits of a brevity that had raised even the doctor's eyebrows.

"You can do what you like in the house—even grease the bannisters," the doctor had said, "but if you *must* cavort about in those *cache-sexes,* for God's sake, stay on the grounds!"

Dr. Robbertson had left early that morning on some errand connected with his marriage. Dirk was still bemused about the affair, wondering whether he'd lose his profitable sittings under the new régime. But, then, if he and Tommy went to London . . . Tommy was absorbed in speculation about his impending aunt and hoping he might get a chance to visit them in Sweden. He'd heard the Swedes weren't uptight about bathing naked in the ocean.

Presently, they tired of tennis and lay down upon the soft grass beside the court. After some moments of silent basking, Dirk turned on his side to look at his young friend.

"Have you noticed that chauffeur over at the Hall? The one who brought us back here, Tommy?"

"Yeh," said Tommy, who had already wondered whether if Cartwright would be interested in a London job.

"Think he bleaches his hair?" asked Dirk.

"Naw—it's too natural. If he did, he'd prob'ly bleach his eyebrows, too. Man, that's some combination!"

"That's what I thought," said Dirk. Then he chuckled. "Let's ask him to have a drink with us. He must think he's in a home for the aged in that place. I feel sorry for the kid."

"Okay by me. *You* ask him."

Lady Mauley looked at Cartwright as he polished the trim of the Daimler.

"We shan't be leaving before Sunday. Will that give you time enough?"

"Oh, yes, m'lady. That'll be perfect."

"Splendid! When you've finished currying that spavined machine, you can consider yourself free until—oh, until about ten o'clock on Sunday morning. I *had* thought of going out to dinner tomorrow night, but if I do, I shall ask Mr. Tunstall to take me in his motor. You'll have Saturday night free in that way."

"Thank you, m'lady," said Cartwright.

Lady Mauley turned to go. Suddenly, she stopped and smiled at Cartwright, who looked very serious and very young as he frowned over his polishing.

"Cartwright?"

"Yes, m'lady?"

"You know, young man, I hope you're not going to be bored to death at Maulcaster. I'm afraid you'll find very few people of your age there."

"Oh, I'll manage, ma'am."

"There's a young man who's in Cherton at the moment, who lives in Pelham Parva, about two miles from Maulcaster House. Would you like to meet him?"

"Why, yes, m'lady," said Cartwright slowly, feeling little enthusiasm for the idea. He didn't feel much at ease with strangers. *Papa* was enough!

"I'll see what I can do. If you see a dark young man on a Vespa, that's he."

Cartwright stared at Lady Mauley.

"Oh—him!" exclaimed, remembering the supper-party guests.

"Do you know him, then?"

"Er—not *yet,* m'lady. I—I've seen him around, I think."

"You'll like him, Cartwright. *Completely* unaffected and a true gentleman."

Cartwright looked startled.

"Yes, young man, I said *gentleman*—even if he does get his living—or part of it—from a garage. There're gentlemen in garages, you know, just as there are in restaurants. Even French ones!"

Cartwright grinned, his mind busy with plans.

"Thank you, m'lady."

"Umgh!"

33

Lady Thelma was sipping a cup of coffee and munching a macaroon when Dobbins announced Mrs. Dodridge.

"Hello, Julia. Did Charles get off?"

"Finally. The poor man! He was quite exhausted."

"Isn't he usually, after a visit to Cherton?" asked Lady Thelma.

"Well," said Mrs. Dodridge, eyeing the coffeepot, "yes, he is. But this was more than exhaustion. He seemed really quite depressed."

Lady Thelma rang for Dobbins and another cup.

"These are good," she said, proferring the plate of macaroons. "Dobbins made up some of her famous almond paste yesterday."

Mrs. Dodridge took two cakes and frowned as she began to nibble.

"Something curious is going on, Thelma."

"What do you mean?"

"Something about the vicar. Charles said he couldn't tell

me. Mr. Staine went to see Charles last night, but I'd fled to bed. Charles volunteered nothing, and, of course, I didn't ask." She shook her head. "Edwards told me that *something* happened at the Hall the other day, but apparently even Birkett doesn't know what it is."

"Good heavens! I didn't think anything ever escaped the noble Birkett!"

"Neither did I, but evidently it has in this case." Mrs. Dodridge paused for a moment to enjoy her macaroon. "I ran into Robbie this morning as I was having my walk. He looked absolutely radiant as he drove past me—waved like a schoolboy and grinned like a Cheshire cat."

"Your similes leave nothing to the imagination, Julia. What was all the puerile waving and feline grinning about?"

"I don't know. When I passed his garden a little while later, Tommy and Dirk were disporting themselves, practically *tout nu,* on the tennis court, but Robbie was nowhere to be seen."

"Maybe Robbie's decided to marry one of them . . ." Lady Thelma paused as Dobbins entered with the cup.

Dobbins's eyes lighted up but she maintained a demure composure, only watching her mistress with the look that signaled *important news.*

"What is it, Dobbins?" asked Lady Thelma, who had long since resigned herself to her servant's intelligence service.

"Why, ma'am, I couldn't help hear what your ladyship was saying about the doctor. If you'll allow me, ma'am, I must say it's clever of your ladyship to've guessed."

"Guessed what?" asked Lady Thelma, puzzled.

"Why, the doctor's marrying, ma'am. Miss Granby, I mean."

There was no vulgar outburst. Lady Thelma merely swallowed, and Mrs. Dodridge lowered her eyes to her cup, trying not to choke. Lady Thelma looked inquisitively at Dobbins.

"Yes, ma'am," Dobbins said, nodding. "It's all over the village. Miss Granby and the doctor."

"Are you sure, Dobbins?" asked her mistress.

"Where did you hear it?" asked Mrs. Dodridge at the same time.

"Mr. Hoare, ma'am. He told me about it when I was shopping this morning. Boudicca, she's going to Sweden with 'em. Lucky girl, that one!"

"Sweden?" repeated Lady Thelma, utterly confused.

"Yes, ma'am. Her—Miss Granby, I mean—and the doctor's going to spend the summer in Sweden, and Boudicca's going with 'em."

Lady Thelma suddenly realized that she was gawking.

"Well," she said, composing her features, "that's most interesting. Thank you for telling us, Dobbins. Will you bring some fresh coffee, please?"

Dobbins left, fully aware of having dropped a bomb.

For several moments, the ladies looked thoughtfully at each other.

"Do you suppose it's really true?" asked Mrs. Dodridge, at length.

"Dobbins's forte is communication, not imagination. And I don't think even *I* could have imagined *this!*"

"It's surprising!"

"Your genius for understatement has always been undisputed, Julia."

"Do you suppose they'll take Tommy along with Boudicca?"

"Philip, I want to leave," said Mrs. Tunstall.

"I must say it's not what I'd expected of our visit, in spite of the way it began. Your brother's enough to depress anyone. What on earth do you suppose has happened?"

"I wish I knew. I've tried to question Agnes, but either she knows nothing or Mother's been at her. *Mother* knows what's going on, I'm sure!"

"She usually does," said Mr. Tunstall. He meditated. "It all began with that wretched visit by the vicar. Did you notice how pale he became when the bishop and Charlie came in?"

"Yes, I did. And Charlie was totally unlike himself. You know how fond he is of those impossible people—and he cut them dead. Absolutely!"

"Obviously, Jean, there's been some sort of blowup."

"Well," said Mrs. Tunstall, "I dare say it'll blow over."

"I dare say it won't," said Lady Mauley, coming into the drawing room.

"All right, Mother. Let's have it. What's going on?"

Lady Mauley glared at her daughter. Then she shrugged. "You'll find out sooner or later. You may as well know."

And, briefly and pointedly, she told them.

"And the vicar said that?" asked Philip Tunstall, his face ruddy.

"My dear Philip, I am, I think, a rather broad-minded old woman, but I shouldn't dream of telling you the rest of what he said. If you wish to put poor Charlie through the embarrassment of repeating the remarks of that unspeakable man, that's up to you. I hope you won't. *N'ai-je donc tant vécu que pour cette infamie?* sums it up succinctly. Charlie has his limitations but deliberate rudeness and a breach of hospitality are not among his failings."

Mrs. Tunstall wondered how her mother would defend the recent cocktail party, but she said nothing.

"But it's outrageous," expostulated Mr. Tunstall. "The man deserves to be defrocked!"

"Charlie is willing to compromise," said Lady Mauley. "All he asks is that the bishop find Mr. Staine another parish."

"Is the bishop willing to do that? After all this, Mother?"

"Y-e-e-s," said Lady Mauley slowly. "The bishop seemed quite willing. It was really rather odd, you know. It seemed almost as if he felt partially responsible."

"Oh, now, Mother! Surely you're imagining things!"

"Possibly. But his manner was decidedly strange."

"Well—" began Mr. Tunstall.

"Hush!" whispered Lady Mauley. "Charlie's coming." And, raising her voice, she said, "That figure of Louis XV is most charming. I can't imagine how Charlie manages to find such delicious bits of china!"

"There's a trunk call from Wroxminster for you, Mr. Staine," said Simms.

The vicar and his wife exchanged timorous glances. Then he left the dining room. Mrs. Staine stared at her soup and absently crumbled bits of a crouton, reliving for the hundredth time the scene in the folly. She started as her husband entered.

"It's all settled, my dear," he said. His wife noticed that his voice had resumed its usual abnormal plangency.

"Settled, Frederick?"

"St. Swithin's—a delightful parish near Pelham Abbas. We shall be quite close to your family."

"Oh, Frederick," said Mrs. Staine rather mournfully.

"The bishop is a man of his word, my dear. He has been commendably prompt."

"Who—whose parish is it?"

"It's in Bishop Grossmith's diocese. The incumbent is a gentleman named Markby. He wants to leave because of his wife's health, the bishop said. I spoke only a short time, of course, but I gather that the vicarage is considerably superior to this one, with a delightful orchard and garden. The bishop wants me to motor up there tomorrow. I shall resign the living here at once."

"Oh, *Frederick!*" exclaimed Mrs. Staine and burst into tears.

"What on earth, Lela!"

"I—I don't *want* to leave Cherton!" she wailed.

34

"Julia? This is Thelma."

"Good heavens, woman! Do you know that it's barely seven o'clock? Why did I ever have a telephone put in my bedroom?"

"Sorry, but I *had* to call you. The vicar's gone to Pelham Abbas."

"And," asked Mrs. Dodridge fretfully, "you woke me out of a sound sleep to tell me *that?*"

"Yes," replied Lady Thelma remorselessly. "There's more than meets the eye, Julia."

"A good deal has been meeting *your* eye, I should say. I'm sorry it wasn't my fist! Just a moment—Edwards, bring me my tea, please. Sorry, Thelma, but at least I can refresh myself while you bring me up to date."

"Yes. I'm having my breakfast now. Can you hear the toast?"

"Thelma, stop being ridiculous, and tell me what it is you have on your—*hah!*—mind."

There was a pause. Mrs. Dodridge felt that her friend was switching on footlights and tapping a baton.

"Well, Thelma?"

"Well, Julia, it seems that Dobbins was talking with Simms, the Staines' Simms, last night at their bridge club. Simms told her that the Staines are going to leave Cherton for Pelham Abbas, that Lela is livid, that Frederick is fretful, and that Lady Mauley has maneuvered the whole matter!"

"Beautifully put, my dear. How long did you practice *that?*"

"Dobbins further said," Lady Thelma continued, ignoring the comment, "that she heard that the vicar was grossly rude to Charlie Mauley and that the bishop and Lady Mauley have arranged an exchange of livings."

"Charles certainly did make any number of mysterious telephone calls," said Mrs. Dodridge. She thought for a moment. "So we're going to have a new vicar?"

"Yes, Julia. Can you imagine it?"

"I shall certainly try very hard, and I forgive you for calling at this ungodly hour. Can *you* imagine what Cherton could be like without the Staines?"

"I've often enough wished to find out. But—it will seem rather odd, won't it, with Fanny and Robbie gone, too?"

"But surely that's only for the summer?"

"I don't know. Dobbins seems to think that they'll not be coming back at all. Young Corelli is apparently going to try to find congenial work in London—whatever *that* means. By the way, Fanny and Robbie are going up to London themselves this morning."

"You've certainly been taken into Dobbins's confidence!"

"Well, you know Dobbins. Give her her head and she's off and away. The facts and surmises pour from her like beer from a pump. In the last forty-eight hours, she's become as communicative as Miss Bates."

"Your similes leave nothing to the imagination, Thelma," said Mrs. Dodridge acidly.

Lady Thelma laughed.

"All right, Julia! I deserved that. But you know, I have an idea that this may be the beginning of a sort of swan song. Cherton may be a very different place—in some respects."

"I can scarcely wait."

"You're most prompt, Stephen. Right on the dot."

"We should be in London with time to spare. I want to take you to a shop in Regent Street before we go to the church."

"Now, dear, you're not going to be extravagent, are you?"

"Not very, Fanny. But there's a little something for you at Garrard's."

"*Garrard's!* You're not extravagant, Stephen. You're completely mad!"

"But it's such fun—being mad."

"Well, I'm ready. The luggage is ready. Boudicca will see that it's sent to Le Drapeau Bleu. Really, the dear girl is almost as excited as I!"

"I'm excited, too," said Dr. Robbertson, smiling. Then he fumbled in his coat pocket. "Fanny, Tommy sent you this."

Miss Granby gravely took the small package.

"How very sweet of him! I'm glad that he thinks so much of me. I think he'll be a nice nephew."

"He's a good lad. I hope that someday he'll be as happy as you've made me."

"I hope so, too, Stephen. We'll have to try to do what we can for him. I hope that eventually he'll let us give him a home."

"I don't know," said the doctor as they settled into the car. "Tommy has an independent spirit—and a good head on his shoulders, believe it or not. He's managed to save an astonishing amount of money, in spite of the expensive tastes he's acquired. Knowing Tommy has been quite an education, Fanny."

Miss Granby pondered as the car moved toward the London road.

"What is Tommy going to do if he doesn't remain with us, Stephen?"

The doctor pursed his lips thoughtfully.

"He wants to try living in London. He's used to a city, and Cherton bores him—as well it might."

"But—but how will he live? Can he live indefinitely on his savings?"

"He's talking about going into—er—trade," said Dr. Robbertson evasively.

"What sort of trade?" asked Miss Granby.

The doctor turned to grin at her.

"You *are* the curious aunt, aren't you? If I tell you, you may wish you hadn't asked."

"Stephen, dear," said Miss Granby patiently, "I'm not completely obtuse, you know. Tommy should do very well, but I hope he'll be careful—and Dirk, too."

"Fanny, is there no end to the shocks you can give me? It'll take me *years* really to know you!"

"Anyway," said Miss Granby, "I hope that both of them will be willing to pay us a visit this summer."

"I think they will. But, Fanny, we're being too serious. This is going to be a wonderful day. Look at that sky! It's glorious for March!"

"Oh, Stephen! It *is* a wonderful day!"

"Mother, I think that I shall go to France."

Lady Mauley raised her eyebrows.

"Where?" she asked.

Lord Mauley considered.

"Paris, first, I think. I want to look at some of the things at the Louvre. Then I rather think that I shall spend a bit of time at Cannes. Jean and Philip will be there next month." Lord Mauley paused. "Mother—Philip has been very good to me lately."

Lady Mauley hesitated.

"Like you, Charlie, Philip has many good qualities. Perhaps it's unfortunate that you both don't have the *same* good qualities, but that we must put up with. Philip could do with some of your good nature, Charlie."

"Perhaps, Mother. But I could do with some of his brains, you know."

"Oh, nonsense, Charlie!"

"I know I'm not clever, Mother."

"I don't know that that's really true," said Lady Mauley cautiously, "but even if it *were,* at least you're clever enough to know it!"

"I think it's true, Mother."

Miss Pollock entered the room in time to view the stupefying spectacle of Lady Mauley kissing her son.

"Oh, Agnes! Did you telephone Le Drapeau Bleu?"

"Yes, Cousin Emily. I told them that we'd be there between seven and eight."

"Splendid! You're coming with us, aren't you, Charlie?"

"I had Birkett call Cook's this morning. I shall be taking the boat train tonight."

"You're leaving for France *today?*"

"I rather think so. Yes, Mother, I am. I—I want to get away."

Lady Mauley said no more, and her expression was such that Miss Pollock said nothing at all.

"Thomas! Have you *heard* about the Staines?"

"What about them?"

"They're *leaving* Cherton!"

Thomas Hitchcock sat up in his chair as if a spring had uncoiled beneath him.

"You don't mean it!"

"Oh, but I *do!* It's all *over* the village!"

"Well, well, *well!*"

"Yes!"

"So old Freddy has finally got his comeuppance!"

"What do you mean, Thomas?"

"Why, it's obvious, isn't it, that this is the result of that episode in the folly last Tuesday? Charlie-boy didn't lose any time!"

"You really think so?"

"I'm sure of it, Portia."

"Oh—you haven't seen Lord Mauley? To—to apologize?"

Thomas Hitchcock waved a pontifical hand.

"No hurry, my dear, no hurry at all. I dare say that in view of the vicar's remarks, Lord Mauley doesn't even remember that we were there."

"Well, I really think that you ought to see him without further delay, Thomas. He may be expecting you to ring or call."

"All in good time, Portia, all in good time. Ah, here's the post!"

Félicité entered with the morning's letters. Mrs. Hitchcock took them and sorted them.

"One from Peggy Langhorne in Bern. About time she replied! Here, this is for you. It looks like Cousin Mary's hand."

"Hmm. So it does. Wonder how the old vulture is."

"The new *Country Life*—lovely, and—*oh!*"

Mr. Hitchcock peered over his spectacles.

"What is it?" he asked.

Mrs. Hitchcock swallowed, staring at the long envelope in her hand.

"It's from Denbigh and Waltham—Lord Mauley's solicitors!"

Her husband turned a regrettable shade of off-white but he managed to reach for the letter.

"Now don't be worried, Portia. They're probably finally replying about the roof for the garage."

"Open it," said Mrs. Hitchcock in a choked voice.

Mr. Hitchcock opened the envelope and unfolded the letter.

"Hell and damnation!"

"Oh, Thomas! What *is* it?"

"A—a Notice to Quit," said Mr. Hitchcock in a low voice.

The letter fluttered to the floor.

"Oh, Thomas, you should have *gone!*"

He attempted to rally.

"I shall go—today. I—I was wrong—or at least I was rather delinquent in not going sooner. I—I'm sure that I can smooth everything over very easily. I shall telephone Lord Mauley to say that I wish to see him."

"Thomas, *do* go *now!* Don't telephone! Go *now!*"

"No, I must have time to think. I must be able to express myself—adequately. Portia, ring for some brandy."

"But it's not *nine* o'clock!"

"I regard this as a medicinal dose. Please call Félicité."

"Mr. Cartwright? Got some luggage 'ere for you. Belongs to a Dr. and Mrs. Robbertson."

"Just set it down there, Parkins. I'll have the boy take it up."

Mrs. Cartwright put her head through the doorway to the dining room.

"Qu'est-ce qu'il y a?"

In a quarter of a century, Mr. Cartwright had acquired but a smattering of French, in spite of the fact that his wife scorned any other tongue.

"Robbertson," he said laconically. *"Leurs valises."*

"Ah, bon! André! André? Où es-tu?"

The "boy," a weary redheaded Scot, appeared. Andrew Lochore picked up the luggage and looked inquiringly at his employers.

"Au premier—la grande chambre," said Mrs. Cartwright.

Lochore stared at her husband.

"First-floor front," said Mr. Cartwright helpfully.

"Vive la France!" muttered Lochore and departed for the upper floor.

Slowly Mr. Hitchcock replaced the telephone and looked haggardly at his wife.

"He left for Paris two hours ago," he said hoarsely.

"Oh, *Thomas!*" exclaimed Mrs. Hitchcock and burst into tears.

35

Dirk, Tommy, and Terry Cartwright descended from the Cherton–Wroxley bus and began to walk up Cobb Street. When, earlier in the day, Dirk had ostensibly accidentally encountered Cartwright in the road before the Hall, Cartwright, managing to overcome his timidity, had broken into Dirk's conversational preliminaries, inviting him and Tommy to have dinner with him at Le Drapeau Bleu. Bemused and nothing loath, Dirk accepted for both, quietly taking inventory of the striking blond youth before him.

Tommy, as well as Dirk, had a remarkable ability to put people at their ease. Cartwright had responded with almost pathetic friendliness, and now, as they trudged through the narrow street, all were pleased.

"Mus' seem funny ta ya, comin' ta ya ol' man's place like this," said Tommy, wanting to make conversation. "He give ya a cut?"

''Shut up!'' growled Dirk between his teeth.

''Huh? Did I say somethin' wrong?''

''It's all right, Tommy,'' said Cartwright amiably. ''Of course I don't have to pay—at least except for the drinks. But, anyhow, remember that you and Dirk are my guests tonight.''

''Yes, Tommy, try to remember that,'' said Dirk, still annoyed. He had a deep affection for his young American friend, but he would have to do something to correct Tommy's tendency to say the wrong thing or to talk at the wrong time—or both.

''Oh, don't scold him, Dirk. He didn't mean anything, did you, Tommy?''

''No,'' said Tommy, subdued. ''I wuz jus' askin'.''

''I hope *Maman* got the ducks she was talking about. *Bigarade!* Wait'll you taste it!''

''Huh?'' said Tommy.

''Roast duck with orange sauce. Then, after the salad, we'll have *tarte aux groseilles,* and—''

"Huh?" said Tommy again.

''What in *hell* are you talking about, Terry?'' asked Dirk with a laugh, his good humor regained. ''Talk English!''

Cartwright laughed in turn.

''Sorry! I get carried away. That's my mother's influence. I was talking about gooseberry tart.''

''Is *that* what that means?'' asked Dirk. ''I thought you were talking about something fancy.''

''I *am!* Wait 'til you taste it, lads! You'll think you've never known how good gooseberries can be!''

Tommy, who loathed gooseberries, said nothing. He was not demanding. A cheeseburger and a chocolate malt would have suited him perfectly. He liked England but he yearned for what he considered honest American food. His mother had been a ''good plain cook'' in the English sense, and, in consequence, he had yet to learn a great deal about food.

''Here we are,'' said Cartwright. He ushered his new friends into the little lobby.

"Ah, chéri! Tu es arrivé! Et ces messieurs? Ce sont tes connaissances?"

Gravely, Cartwright presented Dirk and Tommy—in French, to the latter's bewilderment. Tommy caught Dirk's eye and kept his mouth shut.

Still chattering gaily, Mrs. Cartwright led them to a round table near the cheerful fire in the dining parlor.

"On veut des cocktails, sans doute, messieurs?" she asked.

"Chère Maman, les cocktails ne sont pas dignes de ta cuisine. Nous aurons du Xérès."

"Ah, mon fils, tes amis sont bien *instruits!"*

And Mrs. Cartwright departed, wreathed in smiles.

"What," asked Dirk softly, "did all *that* mean?"

"Do you like sherry?" asked Cartwright cautiously.

"Sure. It's great," said Dirk.

"Tommy? Do you like sherry?"

"Cherry?"

"He'll like it, Terry," said Dirk with a grin. "If it's alcohol, it's okay. Right, Tommy?"

"Yeh. Cherry?"

"Sssh-erry," said Dirk, smiling at Tommy's puzzlement.

"Well!" said Lady Mauley. "Here we are! Agnes, where's my stick? Oh, thank you, my dear."

"My word! I've not been here in donkey's ears," said Mr. Tunstall, assisting his mother-in-law from the car. "The food's still good, is it?"

"It's superb, Philip," said Miss Pollock. "I've never understood why they stay here. They could make a fortune in London."

"Let's be grateful they *are* here," said Lady Mauley. "It's the only place to get a really good dinner for miles around. Why Charlie tolerates the constructions of that mechanic he employs is more than I shall ever understand. Did you taste that meringue last night? I'm sure she puts plaster of Paris in the things!"

"You're spoiled, Mother," said Mrs. Tunstall. "*Jerson* could make a fortune in London, if it comes to that. Why she's content to waste her talents on you and Agnes, I don't know."

"I can assure you, Jean, that she has two most appreciative—ah, *consumers,*" said Lady Mauley complacently, "and if you wonder why she remains with me, the answer is very simple."

"Pure devotion and attachment?" suggested Mr. Tunstall.

"Pure devotion and attachment to the root of all evil. That woman *is* making a fortune—and at my expense. Otherwise, I might be able to put that wretched Daimler out to pasture and order a Silver Ghost."

"I think I prefer having Jerson, Cousin Emily. She's worth it."

"Yes," agreed Lady Mauley. "Are we going to stand on this pavement all night?"

Dr. Robbertson dried his hands and walked back into the attractive little sitting room of Le Drapeau Bleu's best suite.

"There! I feel much better. All that London grime off."

"Stephen, I'm *very* glad we decided to come back here instead of staying over in London. The remoteness and peace are exquisite."

"Wroxley's a pleasant little place. Not so pretty, perhaps, as Cherton."

"No, it's not, but it's a change."

"Quite a few changes today, Mrs. Stephen Robbertson!"

"How lovely that sounds to me! Only, it'll take some getting used to, Stephen. 'Fanny Robbertson'—it's lovely."

"Granby's a pretty name, Fanny."

"I suppose it is. 'The Marquess of Granby.' But with 'Fanny'—it always reminded me of some character out of Jane Austen's books."

"You're not a bit like any Fanny in Jane Austen. One of

them was a sanctimonious little creep-mouse, and the other was a bitch!''

"I don't know any of her books except *Pride and Prejudice,* I'm ashamed to admit."

"It's a good one to begin with. Well, Fanny Price in *Mansfield Park* is the mouse. Fanny Dashwood in *Sense and Sensibility* is the bitch. You must read them, my dear."

"We'll read them together. What fun!"

"It's close to eight. Shall we go down to dinner or have it sent up?"

"Oh, let's go down. I want to flaunt my ring. Really, darling, you *were* extravagant. A plain gold band would have been enough, and here you have me looking like Diamond Lil!"

"Frederick!" exclaimed Mrs. Staine. "I'd no *idea* you'd be back so soon!"

"A very easy trip, my dear Lela, and a most satisfactory arrangement. I feel sure that you will adjust to it without any difficulty whatever."

"Oh?"

"The house is delightful. About 1690. Brick, of course, *and* central heating! The kitchen has been completely renovated in the past year, and, as for the baths, my dear Lela, they look like something in an American film!"

"Is there a garden?"

"*Quite* a garden! Apparently it's been Mrs. Markby's solace. The poor woman is a martyr to the altitude. It's very high and, consequently, rather dry. Lela, I'm certain you'll love it!"

Mrs. Staine smiled bravely and stiffened her upper lip. She looked rather like the Mad Hatter as a result, but her fortitude aroused her husband's admiration.

"We really must celebrate, Lela. Shall we have some of our champagne with dinner?"

"Oh, *Frederick!*" exclaimed Mrs. Staine regretfully. I—I

didn't expect you for dinner, so I let Simms go home. I was just going to have a *sandwich* or something."

"Never mind, my dear Lela, never mind," said the vicar with resonant expansiveness. "Things have worked out so beautifully! This is really a reason for celebration! What do you say to our motoring over to Wroxley? To that excellent little restaurant?"

Mrs. Staine's eyes gleamed.

"The hotel? Le Drapeau Bleu?"

"Precisely."

"Oh, how *too* divine! Why don't you call them while I make myself presentable? I've not been there for *ages!*"

Mrs. Cartwright frowned slightly when Dirk and Tommy lit cigarettes as they began their sherry. Evidently, the young men weren't quite so *bien instruits* as she had thought. Then she shrugged. At least they hadn't tried to order martinis!

Tommy sipped the sherry, a very pale and very dry vintage. At first, he thought it was terrible; then he wasn't so sure. After the third sip, he stared happily across the room at nothing in particular.

Dirk looked down into his glass, admiring the color of the wine and wondering about its power.

Cartwright surveyed his guests with a satisfaction that was becoming warmer by the minute, relieved to find that his misgivings concerning their public behavior were groundless.

Dirk continued to stare into his glass.

"Wonder what Robbie and Miss Granby are doing," he said dreamily.

"Yeh," said Tommy. "Musta made it legal by now."

Cartwright suddenly laughed.

"Whatsa matter?" asked Tommy, surprised.

"Look!" whispered Cartwright, nodding toward the doorway.

Framed in it were Dr. Robbertson, resplendent in an impeccably fitted dinner jacket, and Miss Granby, or rather,

Mrs Robbertson, in a highly becoming gown of a heavy deep-gold silk, with a cluster of bronze orchids at her shoulder.

At the very moment that the six young eyes were turned upon him, Dr. Robbertson saw the trio. He smiled broadly and, turning to his wife, directed her glance to the table.

"Fanny! Look!"

Mrs. Robbertson looked and smiled.

"Let's go speak to them, Stephen."

"We don't have to, you know. We can see Tommy tomorrow."

"Oh, nonsense!" she said, and she crossed to the table by the fireplace.

The youths bounded to their feet, and Cartwright was grateful to his parents for the dim, if romantic, lighting of the room. Was he going to encounter socially every casualty he had driven home from Lady Mauley's party?

"Tommy, my dear! And Dirk!" exclaimed the bride. "Tommy, dear, I've so wanted to thank you for this charming pin. I love it! See? It's holding my flowers." And she put her arms about his neck and kissed him heartily on the cheek.

To the doctor's astonishment, his nephew blushed scarlet. Dr. Robbertson laughed and clapped the boy upon the shoulder.

"Be careful, Tommy! Your aunt is trying to compromise you!" he said, smiling into the boy's eyes.

Tommy muttered grateful incoherencies, and, in mercy, Mrs. Robbertson turned to Dirk.

"Won't you and your friend join us for dinner, Dirk?" she asked.

Dirk merely smiled and introduced Cartwright, who wondered wildly how he had contrived to get into such a situation.

Dr. Robbertson was wondering whether etiquette forbade strangling one's bride on her wedding night, when rescue came from a totally unexpected quarter.

"Uh—Miss Granby—I—mean—Mrs. Robbertson—uh—

Aunt Fanny? It's real nice of ya, but—we couldn't do that. You and Robbie oughta—well, have dinner jus' by ya selves, oughtn't ya? . . . I mean—I wuz lookin' at th' pretty table over there—with all th' flowers an' candles an' things—and—well, I don't think we *oughta,* d'*you,* Dirk?''

Gratefully, Dirk agreed, and a glance at her husband's face persuaded Fanny that she was perhaps overdoing the cordiality act, sincerely though she meant it.

As the Robbertsons crossed to their own table, the three young men sat down. Presently, Dirk shot a furtive look at Tommy.

''Well done!''

''I'll say!'' said Cartwright.

''But it *wuz* nice of her,'' said Tommy, half-smiling.

''Right you are,'' said Dirk. ''She's a real lady.''

''Robbertson's lucky,'' said Cartwright.

To his consternation, he saw Tommy's and Dirk's eyes converging upon him.

''So're we,'' they said in unison, smiling beatifically.

''*Uh!* . . . Have some more wine?'' Cartwright asked hurriedly.

''This way, m'lady,'' said Mr. Cartwright.

''Why, there's Dr. Robbertson! And Miss Granby! What a delightful meeting!'' exclaimed Lady Mauley.

Dr. Robbertson just managed not to choke as he rose to his feet. He could not help admiring his wife's aplomb. There was a flutter of ''So nice to see you again,'' ''Such a lovely day,'' as the Tunstalls, Miss Pollock, and Lady Mauley hovered about the Robbertsons' table. A look from Mrs. Robbertson decided the doctor.

''Lady Mauley,'' he said, ''I should like you to be among the first to share our little surprise. Fanny and I were married at St. Bride's in town this morning.''

The crisis at the Hall had prevented Lady Mauley from hearing the news earlier, but her eyes had already taken in the flowers, the gown, and the diamonds. She extended her hand.

"My congratulations, Doctor! And my dear Fanny! I'm so pleased for you both. You've really been very sly, my dears, and I wish you all the happiness in the world." And she kissed the younger woman.

The Tunstalls were startled enough for the reflexes of long training to take command. Miss Pollock was enjoying her usual reaction to any shock: total numbness.

From the other side of the room the youths watched the scene. At least one of them was trying to contrive getting out without being noticed. It was not their choice that at that moment a couple at an adjoining table were regaled with the illumination of crêpes suzette. The flames of the always fascinating ritual drew the eyes of others to that quarter of the room. Lady Mauley beamed, and the flames of the crêpes seemed to pale.

"Mr. Henderson! *And* Mr. Corelli! How *delightful!*"

"Jesus!" Dirk muttered.

Tommy, however, looked up and, tossing back his hair, waved happily at the group from the Hall.

"Oh, merde!" whispered Cartwright. How much did his new employer *really* know about his even newer friends? Oh, well! *Maman* could always force his father to give him a job!

"And *Cartwright!*" added Lady Mauley, suddenly realizing that her chauffeur was also present. (The young man had lost no time!) Then she herded her muttering, protesting party across the room.

Mrs. Robbertson smiled at her husband.

"At least it's not their wedding supper!" she murmured.

"Umm " said Dr. Robbertson, "no. Not exactly a wedding supper. I think they're just celebrating."

"Celebrating what, Stephen?"

"Oh, perhaps our wedding. Or perhaps just—celebrating."

"Shall we have our pudding and coffee upstairs by our fire, Stephen?"

"Yes!"

By the fireplace, Dirk, Tommy, and Cartwright smiled and smiled and made talk as best they could until Philip Tunstall could stand it no longer.

"Lady Mauley," he said, "I think we're keeping these young men from their dinner."

"Umgh! Yes, I suppose we shouldn't. Well, we'd better sit down. Oh, but why don't we *all*—"

"Mother!"

"Uh—yes, Jean?"

"Do let's sit down at *our* table, *shall* we? I'm famished!"

"So am I!" said Miss Pollock, desperation goading her to speech. "*Really,* Cousin Emily!" she added under her breath.

Lady Mauley sighed. Then she smiled at the perplexed young trio.

"Enjoy your dinner, young men. I hope I shall see you soon again. Since you know Cartwright, you must call on us at Maulcaster. Perhaps you'll be able to come for a visit?"

It was not necessary for the Tunstalls to help Miss Pollock to their table, but for a moment they thought it would be.

The Robbertsons were almost to the door, hoping that they were unnoticed. It was not entirely their lucky night. The Staines were just coming in.

They smiled mechanically at Mrs. Staine, praying that their faces gave no indication of their thoughts.

"Dr. Robbertson! And *Mrs. Stephen Robbertson!* Oh, you *slyboots,* both of you!"

"Slyboots, indeed!" intoned the vicar, pulling out the thirty-two-foot stop. "Why, you were very naughty, you know, not to let me tie the knot!"

Here Mr. Staine laughed jovially, a basso ostinato to his wife's gibbering charm.

Dr. Robbertson said what he could—and that was more than he had thought himself capable of saying. His wife smiled unceasingly and said nothing. At last the doctor could bear no more.

"We're just leaving, but we won't leave you *alone*. Lady Mauley and the Tunstalls are here. Also my friend Dirk Henderson. See? Over there? Across the room?"

And with that, the doctor and his wife fled to the possibly doubtful safety of their suite.

The adult Cartwrights were voluble.

"Made a reservation and everything! Ordered a dinner we've been working on this last hour, and what's he do? Gets in here, stays two minutes, and turns on his heel and walks out! Not a word of explanation! Not even a tip! What're we to do with all that food? That's a fine way for a clergyman to act!"

"Never mind, Father," said Cartwright, who was showing his friends around the kitchen. "Send him a bill for the dinner. When I see you tomorrow, I'll tell you more about him."

"Bloody fool!" growled Mr. Cartwright.

"That he is," said Dirk.

" 'Sa jerk," said Tommy.

"Mes hommages à mademoiselle sa mère!" muttered Mrs. Cartwright.

As the bus drew into Cherton, Dirk, who had been unusually quiet during the trip, turned to Cartwright.

"Why don't you come over for a nightcap, Terry? Do you have to go right back to the Hall?"

"Why," said Cartwright hesitantly, "that would be nice. You sure it'll be convenient?"

"Nobody'll be there 'cept us," said Tommy, wondering somewhat uneasily what Cartwright would think of his uncle's paintings.

"Well, fine!" said Cartwright.

"What's the time?" asked Cartwright groggily.

"Who cares?" asked Tommy, wrapping his legs around Cartwright's.

"It's a little past five, Terry," said Dirk.

"Oh." Cartwright sighed. "I don't want to leave."

"D'ya reely havta, Terry?"

"Well, I guess not. Lady Mauley said I don't have to be there until tomorrow."

"Then you don't have to go," said Dirk, fondling Cartwright's several dependencies.

"Mebbe he oughta come 'steada go," suggested Tommy helpfully.

"Again?" asked Cartwright, still unable to believe his luck and the sense of glorious relief.

Tommy gave a sudden start.

"*Christ,* Dirk!" he cried. "How d'ya *do* it? Oooh! *Jeeeeeze!*"

Dirk's reply was audible but incomprehensible.

"My mom always tol' me not ta talk with my mouth full," Tommy confided to Cartwright, giving an ecstatic wriggle.

"*You* talk too much," said Dirk, stopping momentarily and grinning. "And hold *still,* can't you, *dammit!*"

36

"Philip, have you heard the latest?" asked his wife.

"Probably not, since you look as if I hadn't. What is it?"

"Mother's just told me that the Staines will be leaving in less than a fortnight. It's all settled. He sent his letter of resignation by hand early this morning. Since Charlie's not here, Mother opened it."

"And?"

"She called Bishop Dodridge immediately, and in less than an hour he telephoned to say that Bishop Grossmith is willing to give Pelham Abbas to our dear vicar."

"I take it he doesn't know Staine very well," said Mr. Tunstall with a grin.

"I hope not. I should hate for things to go awry at this stage. And, of course, after this disastrous experience and in a new parish, Mr. Staine may be a little more discreet. He *may* even have learned something, although that seems a trifle farfetched."

"I remember Syd Markby."

"Do you? I don't."

"No, I suppose you wouldn't. I've met him several times on committees in town. A pleasant chap. About Charlie's age, I'd say. He has a sensible wife, too. I think she'll get along very well with Julia Dodridge."

"Well, Philip, it doesn't seem that there'll be very many people left here for her to get along with."

"Hmm. I wonder what impact Staine *will* have on Pelham Abbas."

"I can't imagine."

"Whom is your mother ringing now?"

"Probably Bishop Dodridge. She muttered something about him as she left the table. Oh, hello, Mother."

"Hello, Jean. Umgh! What are you and Philip gossiping about now?"

"Your multifarious telephone conversations."

Lady Mauley grinned.

"I *have* been rather busy. I talked to Sydney Markby after breakfast. I've asked him to drive down so we can all meet him. He should be here very soon now."

"So *we* can meet him?" asked Mrs. Tunstall, puzzled. "Isn't Charlie the one for that?"

"Your brother, Jean, in case you've forgotten it, left for France yesterday."

"I've not forgotten it, but I don't see what *we* can do in the matter."

"It's quite simple. I wish to see if I think Sydney Markby suitable."

"Suppose he isn't?" asked Mr. Tunstall.

"Yes, Mother. Suppose he isn't. What will you do then?"

"Nothing, Jean. However, I wish to be able to write to Charlie that the matter is settled, and I can write more intelligently if I know what the man is like. I've not seen him for some years. He used to be charming."

"He still is," said Philip Tunstall. "Have you met his wife, Lady Mauley?"

"No, but I shall. I've asked him to bring her."

"But the transfer of livings is a fait accompli, isn't it, Mother?"

"Of course."

"Are you going to take Mr. Markby over to meet the vicar?"

"I suppose that I could," said Lady Mauley, trying not to shudder, "but fortunately they've already met—when Mr. Staine went to St. Swithin's yesterday."

"But the wives haven't met, have they, Mother?"

"No, Jean, but it's only a matter of time. The Markbys will be here overnight. I've told him that I'm leaving tomorrow for Maulcaster House. They'll be in the Oak Room."

"Well," said Dirk, loading the last of his portraits onto the Vespa's luggage rack, "I don't suppose we'll be back *here* for a while."

"Mebbe," said Tommy, looking at the doctor's handsome brick house. "I'll kinda miss it. I'm gonna miss Robbie, too."

"I suppose we both will," said Dirk as he tightened the straps.

"And—then—I met *you* in th' house, too."

"That's right, lover," said Dirk with a smile.

Tommy smiled back.

"Is Pelham Abbas closer ta London than Cherton, Dirk?"

"Nope. It's lots farther. Planning to visit Terry?"

Tommy grinned.

"Well, mebbe he could come ta see *us*. It'd be more fun that way when we get a pad."

"We'll stay a few days with Donaldson, the chap who has the agency. He's sure to know of something right for us."

"Mebbe Robbie an' Aunt Fanny'll ask me ta go ta Sweden. I wanna see them—I mean, those nude beaches."

"Maybe I'd better go along to keep an eye on you!"

"Well, hell, Dirk! I wouldn't wanna go jus' by myself."

"By the way, Tommy, I've been meaning to tell you something."

"Somethin' bad?" asked Tommy, his face darkening.

"No, ya silly twit! No, I just wanted to tell you to try not to lose your accent. I can help you straighten up your grammer. So can Donaldson. He talks better than I do, but a lot of people are turned on by a Yank accent."

"I got another idea, too," said Tommy.

"Well, save it for our first stop, luvvy. We've got to get going. Hang on!"

"Well, Elinor, I hope you're going to find the place more comfortable than Pelham Abbas," said Mr. Markby as their Morris rattled over the road into Cherton.

"I hope so, too, Syd. Everyone seems to think that it's very damp, winter and summer. So long as I can begin to breathe again, I don't much care what Cherton is like. The bishop wasn't very explicit, was he?"

"He said that the vicarage has a pretty garden. I've already told you that it's an old house."

"You didn't tell me *how* old," said Mrs. Markby suspiciously.

"About 1500, I think."

"Hot water laid on?"

"I devoutly hope so."

"What about central heating?"

"There isn't any."

"Oh, Lord! I suppose it'll be rheumatism next!"

"You'll have to console yourself, Elinor, with breathing instead of walking."

"I suppose so," said Mrs. Markby, peering through the window. "There's a heavy mist coming on."

"It's four o'clock. We must be nearly there."

The Morris swerved viciously, and Mr. Markby swore deplorably. He brought the car to a violent stop, almost sending his wife through the windscreen. Through the mist, as they scrambled from the car, the Markbys could see a dark object with two figures sprawled beside it. As the Markbys approached, they saw the object to be an ancient Vespa. The two figures rose slowly to their feet.

"I've *told* you, you bloody fool, not to do that to me when I'm driving!" snarled a voice.

"Christ, I'm sorry, Dirk! I didn't mean nothin'," said another voice, with an American accent.

"Look at it! And all the paintings all over everywhere!"

They certainly were. The Markbys gazed in astonishment at some eight or ten smallish canvases strewn about the road. Covered with mud though they were, it was obvious that the artist was well versed in anatomical details of the most virile sort.

"What on earth are you trying to do?" asked Mr. Markby, raging. "Do you know that I very nearly killed you both? To say nothing of ourselves!"

"You drive like a lunatic! You ought to be locked up!" exclaimed his wife, her fright taking the form of anger. Then she stared unbelievingly at the canvases. Suddenly she looked more closely at the black-haired youth confronting her husband and burst into laughter.

"Why—why, they're all *you!*"

"What's that, Elinor?"

"Look, Syd. All these paintings! They're of *him!* Oh, gorgeous!"

Dirk, in spite of himself, felt his face glowing.

"Why don't you carry snapshots of yourself?" asked Mrs. Markby, her good humor restored. "It must be dreadfully inconvenient carting all *these* about. Don't they get in the way?"

Mr. Markby looked at his wife and then at the scarlet youth. For a moment, he tried to maintain his stern manner, but at last he laughed.

"It's my fault, sir," said Tommy, looking uneasily at the Markbys. "I made him lose his balance. He couldn't help it."

"To say nothing of losing the family portraits," said Mrs. Markby.

"I—I'm Dirk Henderson, sir. I'm awfully sorry this happened. I hope you and the lady are all right, sir?"

"I think so," said Mr. Markby more seriously. "*Are* you all right, Elinor?"

"Yes. Quite an introduction to your parish, Syd!"

"Huh?" said Dirk.

"I'm the new vicar here—at Cherton. My name's Markby."

Dirk and Tommy looked at each other, their mouths open.

"Well, there seems to be no harm done. I suppose I ought to report you, but I'll forget it this time. You drive more carefully, young man."

Mrs. Markby looked at the youths, who were still standing as if petrified.

"I think they've gone into trance, Syd."

"Did you hear me, young man?" asked Mr. Markby.

Dirk recollected himself with a jerk of his body.

"Oh—yes, sir. Er—*lots* of luck, Mr. Markby. You—you'll just *love* Cherton!"

Then Dirk and Tommy began to collect the paintings, and the Markbys returned to their car.

"Do you suppose he's one of your parishioners, Syd?"

Mr. Markby did not reply.

"It's getting quite cold. I hope that we have a good tea," his wife continued.

At length Mr. Markby spoke.

"I wonder who painted those pictures," he said.

"*I* wonder *why,*" said his wife.

37

"And *this* is the larder," said Mrs. Staine, throwing open the door and smiling winsomely.

Mrs. Markby noted the condensation upon various objects and glanced up at a large brown spot on the ceiling.

"It's rather *damp,* I'm afraid," said Mrs. Staine apologetically, "but it soon dries out in summer weather."

"Do you ever *have* summer weather in Cherton, Mrs. Staine?"

"Well, occasionally we do—in the *summer,* I mean."

"Oh," said Mrs. Markby, raising her eyebrows, "in the summer."

"Yes. So seasonable, isn't it?"

"What's *that* door?" asked Mrs. Markby.

"Oh, that's the cellar. Would you like to go down?"

"No, thank you," said Mrs. Markby, repressing a shudder. She pointed to another door. "Where does that lead, Mrs. Staine?"

"Oh, that's closed off now. It used to go to the other cellar."

"The other cellar?"

"Yes. It's *under* the house," explained Mrs. Staine.

"What?"

"I—I mean, it's *completely* below the ground—there's no way to get into it now from the outside—except the coal chute, of course."

"I see. Do—do you and Mr. Staine often use the coal chute?"

"Well, only for *coal,* you know," said Mrs. Staine with another smile.

Mrs. Markby decided that an architect might be able to explain the matter and she pulled her coat more closely about her. "Might we go back to the drawing room, Mrs. Staine? You have such a good fire there."

"Oh, of course! I *love* an open fire, don't you? I love to have it in the fireplace."

"That's certainly the best place for it," said Mrs. Markby desperately.

Mr. Staine was showing his successor about the church. Mrs. Markby had flatly refused to enter that beautiful but damp and unheated building. It would be necessary soon enough. She now regretted her decision to see the house instead.

"Would you like tea?" asked Mrs. Staine, although it was nearly half-past six.

Mrs. Markby had reached the end of her patience. It had begun to wear thin when her guide started the Grand Tour by climbing two flights of narrow stairs to the attics and a worm-eaten ladder to the slippery dripping leads.

"Tea?" she said, in the tone with which someone might reject haggis. "I—I wonder if it would be at all possible for me to have a little whiskey? With hot water and lemon? I hope you won't think me rude, but I'm terribly susceptible to double pneumonia."

"Oh! Of *course!* Just—just let me see to it, *dear* Mrs. Markby!"

"Well, Elinor, what did you think of Mrs. Staine?"

"Do you *really* want me to tell you, Syd?"

"Oh, dear!"

38

"Rather an improvement on Frederick Staine," said Mr. Tunstall, returning to the drawing room the Markbys had just quitted. "It's a brilliant morning. I hope they enjoy their trip back."

"I marvel at your moderation, Philip," said Mrs. Tunstall. "Cherton won't be the same, will it?"

"No," said Lady Mauley fervently, "it won't!" She looked about. "Where's Agnes? We're to leave in twenty minutes."

"I'm here, Cousin Emily," said Miss Pollock from a window embrasure. "We're fortunate to have good weather for our own trip." She paused and then added, "Whittaker's taken those two notes, by the way."

"Good!" said Lady Mauley, smiling faintly.

"Perhaps you'll run into young Henderson," said Philip Tunstall maliciously.

"*What* a pleasant young man! And Mr. Corelli, too! And what an amusing encounter with Sydney Markby!" exclaimed Lady Mauley.

"Henderson seems rather given to amusing encounters. Really, Mother, I think that you're going to miss Cherton!"

"With Henderson and Staine within three miles of each other," said Mr. Tunstall, "there's every possibility for a long summer of frivolous collisions—or do I mean collisive frivolities?"

"Mr. Henderson will be in London," said Lady Mauley, drawing on her gloves. "There's Cartwright, Agnes. Are you ready?" Lady Mauley mused. "I think that we must arrange a house party—a long, long house party."

"Cousin Emily!"

Mrs. Dodridge entered the dining room unannounced as Lady Thelma brooded over her breakfast.

Lady Thelma looked at her and groaned.

"Oh, my God! Florence Nightingale and her little lamp of sunshine!"

"Well, yes, I am, rather. I just met Portia at the greengrocer's."

"And what has Dracula's Daughter been up to?"

"She looked perfectly ghastly."

"She usually does. *Well?*"

"Thelma, this will astonish even you!"

"Why 'even' me? Am I so blasé as that?"

Mrs. Dodridge picked up a piece of toast, buttered it, helped herself to guava jelly, and chewed happily, grinning at her friend.

"Oh, all right, Julia! Tell me!"

"The Hitchcocks have received a Notice to Quit."

"What do you mean?"

"I mean that Charlie Mauley has evicted them—cast them forth, as it were."

"What?"

"Exactly what *I* said."

"But—*why?*"

"I wish I knew. All I could make out is that it was somehow connected with the vicar's impending departure, that Thomas has been *dreadfully* misunderstood, that perhaps Heaven Sends These Things as a *Trial,* and that no one knows *where* to turn these days when Buffeted by the Cold Winds of Adversity."

"Julia, you're driveling."

"Naturally. I'm quoting Portia."

Lady Thelma slowly shook her head.

"It's incredible," she said at last. "Robbie, Fanny, the Staines—and now this."

"Cherton is finally changing," remarked Mrs. Dodridge, pouring herself a cup of coffee. "Evidently the Hitchcocks are going to leave the village."

"But changing for the better?"

"Well—possibly."

"Cherton's always been different, hasn't it?"

"And now it's going to be different from what it *was,*" said Mrs. Dodridge. She thought for a moment. "As a matter of fact, it's already different from what it was. It's been changing right under our noses. Do you remember what I said about our needing some kind of shock treatment?"

"Catalysis?" asked Lady Thelma.

Mrs. Dodridge nodded.

"We've been undergoing it without realizing it. I don't think anyone in our little circle has escaped. That dreadful cocktail party!"

"Still worried about that Chinese vase, Julia?"

"*Please,* Thelma! I—I'm sure it was a nightmare."

"I just wondered," said Lady Thelma, once again restraining her curiosity. She lit a cigarette. "I'm not conscious of any particular change in myself, but certainly life here is not going to be the same for you and me. It will seem very odd to have another vicar, won't it?"

"Odd and—I hope—delightful." Mrs. Dodridge considered. "I think it all began—the changes, I mean—with Lady Mauley's arrival."

"Well, *she's* certainly still the same!" said Lady Thelma.

"I wonder if she really is. But, even if she's still the same, isn't that characteristic of a catalyst? Our molecules, as it were, have been rearranged while she's calmly remained on Olympus, pulling the strings."

"I think your metaphor's a trifle mixed, Julia, but I believe you're right. I've always thought, you know, that she deliberately planned that disastrous afternoon on the terrace. I'm beginning to wonder now if she didn't plan a great deal more. The party may not be entirely responsible *directly* but it may have set off a chain reaction. It was Charlie Mauley's bash in the bath that brought his mother down here, you know."

Lady Thelma paused as Dobbins entered.

"This just came from the Hall, ma'am," said Dobbins, indicating an envelope upon a salver.

Lady Thelma and Mrs. Dodridge exchanged glances as Dobbins withdrew.

"Well, for heaven's sake, Thelma! Open it!"

Lady Thelma stared at the envelope.

"I'm not sure that I want to," she said slowly. Then she shrugged and broke the seal. Mrs. Dodridge waited impatiently as her friend read the enclosed letter. Finally Lady Thelma raised her eyes to Mrs. Dodridge.

"Of course it's from Lady Mauley. She writes that she's sorry she had no further opportunity to see me before leaving, but she hopes I'll be able to come to Maulcaster House next month."

Mrs. Dodridge raised her eyebrows.

"Is that all?" she asked.

"Far from it. She goes on to say that there's to be a small party of 'congenial old friends' and that she'll telephone in a few days. Umm. She hopes, by the way, that you'll be able to join us. Evidently she's written to you, too."

"Thelma, I don't like it."

"It's ominous, Julia."

"You're not going, of course?"

Lady Thelma looked glum.

"I certainly don't *intend* to accept—but then I didn't intend to go to that cocktail party, either."

"Thelma, you're mad. Why—what are you going to do? Where are you going?"

"I'm going to call my travel agent in London. I'm taking the first plane to Rome that I can get!"

"You're not serious!"

"Oh, but I *am* serious! I can't cope with any further reactions, chain or otherwise!"

Lady Thelma almost hurled herself through the door, shutting it violently behind her. Left alone, Mrs. Dodridge smiled.

"So it goes right on—just as intended, I suppose." She rose in sudden decision. "After all," she said to herself, "why shouldn't *I* go to Rome with Thelma?"

She crossed the room and went to join her friend at the telephone.

Tommy's fingers rippled over the naked body beside him.

"Umm!" said Dirk, opening his eyes with some difficulty. The previous evening had been a lively one, and even the London daylight seemed blinding. Furthermore, he was still startled by Tommy's uncanny ability to persuade a john to part with fifty pounds and then to enjoy giving the john his money's worth over a period of six hours.

"Wanna be my manager? Fifty-fifty?"

"Hunh?" asked Dirk, his financial sense providing instant alertness.

"Yeh. I'm not on ta th' ropes here. I can't tell if a English guy's gay or not. There's lotsa nice guys in England—an' Swedes are reel dolls. You find 'em, an' I'll service 'em. An' if we both lay 'em, double th' rate. How 'bout it, honey?"

"Fifty-fifty, huh?"

"Yeh. We'll put it in writin'."

Dirk snuggled closer.

"It's a deal. You seem to be as good with the johns as you are with me. Maybe I ought to be jealous, but business is business. Only—do you think you can hold up under the strain, Tommy?"

"Never had no problems in Syracuse," said Tommy, fondling his manager.

Dirk sighed with several varieties of satisfaction.

"Know something, love?"

"Whut?"

"Whores are the only honest people."

"Aw, come off it, Dirk!"

"That's right."

"Whut about Robbie an' Aunt Fanny? An' th' bishop an'—an' Terry an' Lady Mauley? Doncha think *they're* on th' level?"

"Oh, sure. But Terry's our sort. We've got to get him in on this gold mine. Think he'd be interested?"

"Mebbe, but he doesn't have no experience."

"Hell, Tommy! You'd never know it from the other night!"

"No," Tommy admitted. "For a comin'-out party, Terry wuz reel cool, wuzn't he?"

"And he can cook, too, Tommy. Did you know that?"

"Yeh, I heard him when ya thought I wuz asleep. Mebbe we could offer th' johns a—a 'top-hole'?—dinner first. Special dee lukes rates, sorta."

Dirk looked admiringly at Tommy.

"And it'd be fifty-fifty with *him, too?*" he asked.

"Sure."

"I'll get hold of him today, even if I have to drive to Pelham Abbas to do it!"

Tommy was still bothered by his friend's position on honesty.

"Whut *about* th' bishop—an' the others? They *are* on th' level, Dirk!"

"Oh, sure they are, love, but they're confused."

Tommy raised himself on one elbow to stare into Dirk's face. Then he gave a little sigh and lay down again.

"*They're* confused, huh? Okay. Un—mebbe ya jus' better save ya brain fa' business, huh?"

"Do you mean, Cousin Emily, that after less than a fortnight, Cartwright has given notice?"

"A month's notice, Agnes, as is proper. He has found a position in London as a chef, he tells me. He seems to think that he will have the opportunity to serve a 'very discriminating clientele,' as he put it. After all, Agnes, my whole aim in offering him employment was to give him time to decide if he really wanted to abandon *la haute cuisine*. Jerson tells me that he's remarkable. She says he's already given her some new ideas. That marvelous *veau en croûte* we had last night was one of Cartwright's recipes."

"Are you still determined to have that 'small party of congenial old friends,' Cousin Emily?" Miss Pollock asked warily.

"Of course! I shall have to defer it, however. I find that Thelma and Julia have gone to Italy. Fortunately, Julia's servant was able to give me the address. I'm going to write to them now."

"Are they going to be gone long?"

"Only a fortnight or so," said Lady Mauley, taking a sheet of paper from her writing desk. Her pen hovered over the paper as she looked speculatively at Miss Pollock.

"I wonder if Thelma was really serious about young Corelli. *Such* a delightful young man! Of course, she probably wasn't, but perhaps I should just *hint* that he and that handsome Mr. Henderson—"

"Cousin Emily!"